Gwen Reaper

A Young Adult Paranormal Romance

Jaz Primo

RUTHERFORD LITERARY GROUP

www.rutherfordliterary.com

Novels by Jaz Primo

Gwen Reaper
(A Young Adult Paranormal Romance)
Winner of the Paranormal Romance Guild's Reviewer's
Choice Award for Best Young Adult Novel of 2012!

* * *

The Logan Bringer Urban Fantasy Series
Bringer of Fire
Bringer Unleashed **
Bringer's Law **

** Additional Titles Forthcoming

* * *

The Sunset Vampire Series
Sunrise at Sunset
A Bloody London Sunset
Summit at Sunset
Wicked Sunset
Sunset Rising **

** Additional Titles Forthcoming

* * *

All titles published by Rutherford Literary Group

This is a work of fiction. Names, characters, places, and incidents either are the product of the author's imagination or are used fictitiously, and any resemblance to actual persons, living or dead, business establishments, events, or locales is entirely coincidental. The publisher does not have any control over and does not assume any responsibility for author or third-party websites or their content. Any trademarks mentioned herein are not authorized by the trademark owners and do not in any way mean the work is sponsored by or associated with the trademark owners. Any trademarks used are specifically in a descriptive capacity.

Published by:
Rutherford Literary Group
1205 S. Air Depot, PMB #135
Midwest City, OK 73110-4807

Cover art by Sharon Legg
Edited by Lea Ellen Borg
Copyright © 2012 by John Primo
All rights reserved.

ISBN 0982861370
ISBN-13 978-0982861370

DEDICATION

To all those who find love in unexpected places and under
strange or unique circumstances.

JAZ PRIMO

CONTENTS

ACKNOWLEDGMENTS

My love and thanks to my wife, Lori, for all of her continued love, encouragement, and support. And thanks to Selina for voicing her opinions and insights in the only manner she knows.

I issue my special thanks to fellow paranormal romance author, Jamie Magee, for challenging and encouraging me to write a young adult paranormal romance from a young male protagonist's perspective.

I offer a hearty thank you to my creative, gifted, and impressive cover artist, Sharon Legg, for the beautiful cover art on this novel. The haunting image of Gwen is brought to life through your artistry. Thank you to my talented and wonderful editor, Lea Ellen Borg, for her amazing editing skills and keen eye for detail. I gained numerous insights into proper writing technique from you on this project. With each completed novel, I continue to hone my writing craft and talents.

Finally, thank you to all of my friends and fans who continue to be wonderfully supportive of my literary endeavors. While writing is a highly personal experience, it is equally rewarding to share my novels with those who experience enjoyment reading them.

CHAPTER 1

"A thing of beauty is a joy forever: its loveliness increases; it will never pass into nothingness." John Keats, English romantic poet

I never thought that my first exposure to real beauty would be tinged with the threat of oblivion...

* * *

"This is just *perfect!*" I complained. "I finally have a steady girlfriend and I'm finally eligible for a starting spot as a safety on our football team."

If my girlfriend, Kelli, got half as upset as I was about it, then she was going to throw a fit. She wasn't very fond of surprises. Kelli liked predictability so much that she had already been talking to her friends about what to wear to prom; and that was next spring, almost a year away.

"Listen, son," Dad said. "Life is just fickle sometimes, so you have to roll with the punches. Besides, we're going to a smaller town that just might need a talented big-city safety on their team. Think of this as an opportunity."

I immediately turned to mom, hoping against fate that she might side with me.

"Life isn't always perfect, Scott," Mom said. "We're all making sacrifices with this move, you know."

Thanks a lot, Mom.

Somehow, I knew it; Dad had already gotten to her.

It was ironic how life occasionally felt like it was destined for perfection. It was in those fleeting moments that I thought that my life was close to being complete. In fact, I wanted the world to freeze in place so that such moments would last forever.

Sometimes those feelings of near perfection lasted for a few hours. Other times they lasted for a few days. On rare occasions, they continued for a couple of weeks. But eventually, something happened to upset the balance, and those sensational feelings, like life, returned to being unfair, unbearable…or worse.

Life was definitely fickle.

My late paternal grandmother, Edna Blackstone, used to say that both things and people were fickle. Not long after grandmother passed away, my dad mysteriously began using that same word.

I wondered if that was destined to happen to me. I hoped not. It was a lame word, in actuality.

Fickle was an old word; one that I had to Google. It meant changeable, or likely to change, especially in affections. By the time I'd turned sixteen, I had determined that fickle was an excellent word to summarize the truth about life. Though not long after that declaration, Mom had chastised me that I was too young to come to that conclusion.

However, I knew better.

My grandmother had died in March, leaving her

hometown business, a grocery store and a convenience store gas station, to her only son; my dad. As if that hadn't been bad enough, Dad said that he didn't have the heart to sell the businesses outright, and instead, he wanted Mom and me to consider the idea of relocating. At first, I was confident that my mother shared the same level of abhorrence that I had.

Then over the period of a couple of months, I could feel the wind shift in the opposite direction, accompanied by a dire sense of inevitability.

In the end, less than a month from starting my junior year in high school, we moved from bustling Springfield, Illinois to the exponentially smaller town of Custer, South Dakota.

Craptastic.

Custer was located 40 miles southwest of Rapid City, the state's second largest city. I liked large cities. Unfortunately, Custer was thirty-fourth on the list with a population of less than three thousand people, not counting the tourists who passed through on their way to see Mount Rushmore.

The town was so small that it seemed like I could throw a rock from the 'Entering Custer' sign at one end of town, and hit the 'Leaving Custer' sign at the other. I had spent only brief periods of time visiting Grandma Blackstone when I was a lot younger; at most, a week during the summers when Dad insisted that we visit. As I got older, I spent more time visiting my mother's parents, Grandpa and Grandma Rogers, who lived just outside Springfield.

After the movers unloaded our furniture and countless boxes and containers, two weeks passed as we unpacked. One of those mornings, I went to enroll for my junior year at Custer High School. I also had to take a computer-based placement test to gauge my aptitude in math and English.

Some people I knew liked tests. I wasn't one of them.

At least the results were immediate, and I did well enough that the school processed my concurrent enrollment in advanced geometry and American Literature courses at Black Hills State University. It was northwest of Rapid City, and was quite a drive from Custer. Fortunately, I was able to attend the courses online.

Given the placement tests, it took most of the day to enroll in school. But by evening, everything had been taken care of.

Great, I thought. *Now I'm a fighting Wildcat.*

Not that they had a large athletics program to speak of. At least Custer actually had a football team, though there were only six teams in the league! The league was merely two-thirds the size of my old high school team, the Springfield Senators, which had been a nine-team league. Add to that, it appeared from last season's standings that the team's performance was erratic, often winning by four touchdowns one week only to lose by that same amount or more the next. The smaller league seemed to lack much parity.

Once my initial surprise over the diminished league size had worn off, I was left with the hopeful notion that at least my football career hadn't abruptly ended before it'd even gotten started. I only hoped that I'd have a chance to try out for the team.

"See? I told you that they had a football team that might benefit from your experience," Dad replied simply, after I shared the news with him.

Mom, on the other hand, was more encouraging, and said, "Trust me, Scott. Your father and I have both seen you play, and I just know that you're going to impress the coach."

Then she gave my dad a hard look.

"Your mother's absolutely right, Scott," he said. "Show them your moves, and you're headed for greatness."

I caught a glimpse of Mom rolling her eyes at him.

"What, Jean?" Dad innocently asked.

Of small consolation, though more likely as a result of my continued disappointment regarding leaving Springfield, was a tidbit of encouragement that I'd been granted. A week after our arrival, Dad surprised me by buying me a relatively new red Chevrolet Blazer at one of the town's used car dealerships. We'd decided to sell my old Ford truck before we moved from Springfield, and I was happy to have a set of wheels again.

"This isn't a bribe, Scott," Dad cautioned me. "Consider this as an inheritance gift from your grandmother."

Either way, it was really kind of Dad to do that for me, and I gave him a hug with my thanks.

The Blazer's body was in pretty good shape, it had a relatively new set of tires, and the engine appeared well-maintained. Best of all, the Blazer's stereo was already equipped with a port so that I could plug my iPod into it.

Cruising with tunes went hand-in-hand for me.

The day after we bought my SUV, I changed the oil in it and gave it a good cleaning, including wiping down the engine with some grease removal solution from the town's only auto part store. Afterward, Dad complimented me on my work and recommended that I take a ride out east to check out the two closest lakes, Bismark and Stockade.

"Hey, if you'll scope out some good fishing spots for us, we'll go this weekend," Dad had said. "And find out where we need to pick up fishing licenses, too."

Within the hour, I was driving along Stockade Lake Drive listening to GROUPLOVE's *Colours* album and appreciating the warm sunshine. Granted, Custer was way too small for my tastes, but the area was scenic beyond belief. Campgrounds and lodges were all over the place, and you could barely look in any direction without laying eyes on a vacationer.

Tourism was the town's lifeblood.

Stockade Lake was breathtaking to behold. Its waters looked clear and blue against the cloudless sky. A seemingly endless blanket of green trees covered the area around the lake. I pulled onto a small dirt road that led from the main road and preceded further back into the trees so that I could get closer to the lake.

A small clearing appeared. I got out of the Blazer to walk to the shoreline. The cool breeze felt refreshing as I surveyed the lake. The shoreline proceeded into a small inlet that led back into the trees; likely a great spot for bass and crappie.

I was convinced that I'd found the first fishing spot for my dad and me to try.

As I walked along the shoreline to get a better look back into the inlet, I saw a girl standing on a small section of beach on the other side of the inlet. She appeared to be about my age, and had long, dark hair and a cute body. It appeared that she was looking at a huge log lying partially out of the water.

Then I realized that the 'huge log' had stubby legs and a snout!

The beast was easily twice her size and weight, and the hulking creature opened its mouth, revealing a long row of teeth. I was fairly sure that it was an alligator or crocodile. But instead of running away, the girl just stood before it, pointing her arm at it like a rod.

"Get away from it!" I called out in warning.

I grabbed a nearby piece of driftwood and started

running toward her. Before I made it ten yards, the creature had thrashed its head and backed away from her, darting backward and disappearing into the water. The girl looked up with surprise to stare at me, and then disappeared into the trees at a dead run.

"Wait!" I yelled, running down the shoreline toward her.

When I got to where she'd been standing, all that I saw were tracks in the sand; both hers and the animal's footprints. I grabbed my cell phone to take photos of the creature's prints, but the lapping water had already partially obscured them, rendering the images relatively useless.

"What the hell was that all about?" I asked incredulously while scanning the trees, hoping that the girl might just be hiding nearby.

Unfortunately, she was gone.

And while I was hardly a reptile expert, I was sure that there weren't supposed to be wild alligators skulking around South Dakota.

* * *

I barely remembered the drive back to town as my mind kept replaying the scene from the lake. What I had seen made no sense for a number of reasons.

When I got home, there was a note on the refrigerator from mom saying that she and dad had gone to the grocery store to look in on things and would return soon. It was still odd to consider that my dad owned a grocery store…and a convenience store, no less.

Life was strange sometimes.

I ran upstairs and started Googling alligators. What I quickly confirmed was that alligators, or crocodiles for that matter, weren't native to South Dakota. However, according to the information I found, there was an extinct species of alligator called alligator prenasalis, of which some fossils had been found in the Oligocene Chadron and Brule Formations in South Dakota.

Based upon what I could recall, and after comparing a host of online photos, I was convinced that the creature that I'd seen certainly appeared to be an alligator. Further searching also revealed that there was a local host of alligators at a place called Reptile Gardens that was located in the Black Hills of South Dakota, just a few miles south of Rapid City. That was less than an hour's drive away from Custer.

Okay, so there were some live alligators not far from Custer, though they were technically supposed to be in a controlled habitat. So, maybe what I'd seen was nothing more than an escaped alligator. That still didn't explain how that girl had somehow influenced the beast.

Why hadn't it attacked her?

Maybe it was a trained pet or something. That might make sense, I suppose.

But what kind of girl would own a pet alligator?

Maybe her parents were wildlife experts or circus freaks.

That prospect seemed pretty cool, actually.

There was no doubt that I was as captivated by the strange girl as much as the alligator.

CHAPTER 2

The weather was perfect on that early Saturday morning as Dad and I arrived at Stockade Lake. I'd picked out a number of prospective fishing locations for us to try, but the first on my list was where I'd seen the girl. Not surprising, though still disappointing, the inlet was devoid of either the girl or the alligator. Still, the fishing was great, and I caught three bass within the first hour of our arrival. They were definitely keepers, too.

I missed Springfield a lot, especially Grandpa Blackstone, who liked fishing and would have loved Stockade Lake. Still, I had to admit that despite its small, nearly claustrophobic size, Custer definitely had its appeal.

But the jury was still out on my final verdict. Actually, it still felt like this place was going to be a tough sell for me; there were just so many unknowns. For example, I wondered if I would like anybody I met at school on Monday.

I missed my old friends back in Springfield. Thus far, I'd kept in touch via texting and Facebook, but it just wasn't the same as having them in town. It felt like my whole life had been upended, and I tried not to feel resentful toward Dad for dragging us to Custer.

By the time we stopped for lunch, Dad and I had caught nearly a dozen keepers; definitely enough for a fish fry that night. Mom had made sandwiches for us, and had packed two pieces of chocolate pie for us.

I loved chocolate.

"Man, this is great pie," I said.

It was so sweet, and it practically melted in my mouth.

"As if I didn't believe the other two times that you said so. It's from Betty's Bakery in town," Dad replied. "Ever since I was growing up, nobody beat Betty's recipes."

"Better not let Mom hear you say that," I said.

He grinned.

"I don't. But then, I also love your mother's baking," he said. "Still, she also knows how much I brag about Betty's creations."

He held up what was left of his pie slice.

"Hence, we have these today," he added with a wink.

Mom was a great cook, but I had to admit that this pie was one notch above amazing in my book.

"Dad, why was it so important for us to move here?" I asked.

I hated to ruin the moment, but I just couldn't understand why our life in Springfield had been so easy for him to want to leave.

Dad thoughtfully regarded me, and sighed in uncustomary fashion.

"I know that it's probably hard for you to understand," he began. "After your Grandma passed away, I just couldn't stand the idea of the family businesses being sold. I realize that the convenience store has only been in our name for less than a decade, but the grocery store is sort of a community symbol."

"But you could've still owned them and let someone here manage them," I said.

"It's not the same, Scott," he said. "This town has been a part of my family for generations. Mom and Dad ran the business together, in fact. It was something that she and Dad always did as a family. They loved it; it was in their blood. After my father died years ago, it was impressive how mom ran everything firsthand up until the week that she passed away. I wanted to experience that for myself."

I considered that for a moment.

"But, Mom's already a nurse," I said. "And I don't see her running a grocery store, much less the convenience store."

"True," Dad conceded. "But maybe it's something that you'd be interested in doing someday."

I stared back at him incredulously. There was no way that I planned to run a small-town grocery store and convenience store for a career.

"Not really my thing, Dad," I said simply.

He shrugged.

"Maybe not today," he conceded. "But who knows how you might feel in a few years. Even in bad economies, people need food and fuel. Custer's so small that it's unlikely that a Walmart is going to move in here any day soon. And the nearest major city is nearly an hour's drive away. Besides, our family business has done well for generations, which enabled my parents to put me through college, as well as save some money for a rainy day. Just consider that only a portion of the inheritance from your grandmother, provided us with the ability to purchase our new house outright, including paying for your Blazer."

That might be true, and I respected Dad's opinion, but living in Custer still didn't sound all that appealing to me. And I couldn't imagine anything that would make me want to stick around after graduation.

Seeing more of the rest of the world sounded a whole lot more interesting to me. At the very least, I imagined going to a large college near a major city somewhere.

"Sure, I get it," I said, mainly to avoid an argument.

We fished into the late afternoon and had a great time. I avoided any further conversation about moving to Custer, and instead just enjoyed the time spent with Dad. And despite the relatively large number of people visiting the lake that day, I failed to spot the dark-haired girl. For that matter,

I didn't catch sight of the alligator, either.

* * *

After sleeping in on Sunday morning, my first thought upon waking was of the amazing chocolate pie that I'd eaten at the lake on Saturday. After a quick workout with the weights that my dad and I had set up in the garage, my focus returned to food. I threw on some jeans and T-shirt, and walked the short distance from our house on Third Street to Mount Rushmore Road, the main street in Custer that was also referred to as Custer Street.

I entered Betty's Bakery & Café to find that the place was bustling with activity, and nearly every table had been taken. I half-considered turning around to leave. But I really wanted a cold Coke, sandwich, and a slice of Betty's amazing chocolate cream pie, so I stood in line, all the while searching the glass display case for the object of my obsession.

When it was my turn at the counter, the grandmotherly-looking woman gave me a long appraising look as I rattled off my selection.

"You're Robert Blackstone's son, aren't you?" she asked.

"Yeah," I replied, noting that a number of heads had turned to stare at me. "I'm Scott."

"You're a spitting image of your father. I can't help but look at that older photo of you and your father on the wall behind the customer service desk at your family's store every time that I cash a check," she said.

Checks? Who still cashes checks?

I politely smiled back at her as I paid for my food and walked around the corner to the main part of the small seating area with tray in hand. As I'd feared, all of the tables were full. I momentarily considered returning to the counter for a to-go box.

Then my eye caught the attractive dark-haired girl who I'd seen while exploring the lake the previous week. She was sitting alone in the corner booth at the back of the room staring at an eBook reader. Her bare legs were stretched out before her with her feet crossed at the ankles in the booth across from her.

As Maroon 5's "She Will Be Loved" played over the café's speaker system, I made my way over to her table.

"Hi," I offered in a friendly overture. "I noticed that the tables are all full, so would you mind if I joined you?" She didn't even look up at me. Her long dark hair cascaded down across the right side of her features like a shield that screamed, 'Go away.' Then I saw the cord leading up to her face from the smartphone on the table before her.

Balancing my tray with one arm, I slowly waved my right hand in front of her to get her attention.

She jolted and glared up at me like I was preparing to attack her.

Despite the pensive look in her vivid blue eyes, I couldn't help but stare back at her with fascination. Her eyes were beautiful.

"What?" she sharply demanded as she withdrew the buds from her ears.

I tried to appear nonchalant as I restated, "Would you mind sharing your table?"

Okay, that sounded a lot less smooth than I'd planned.

"*You*," she whispered in a semi-accusatory tone.

It seemed that she remembered seeing me at the lake, as well; though her reaction suggested to me that wasn't such a good thing.

"I know why you want to sit here, and the answer is *no*," she said.

"Okay," I replied. "It's awfully rude of you, considering the dining room is full. But I can always take this to go."

She frowned and quickly scanned the room. Then she sighed as her delicate shoulders slumped forward slightly.

"Whatever," she said with disappointment as she withdrew her feet from the booth across from her. "I was just leaving anyway."

As she started to collect her phone, I insisted, "Hey,

don't leave. I won't bother you."

She frowned, suspiciously regarded me, and shrugged.

"Fine, but we're not here together," she cautioned as she settled back on her seat and reinserted her ear buds. She quickly returned her attention to her eBook reader.

I sat down, noting that we had garnered a lot of attention from others.

Staring at her, all that I wanted to ask was 'what was that alligator business all about at the lake?'

However, I had the feeling that she was already prepared to bolt from the table as it was, so I decided to play it cool for the time being.

"I'm Scott," I offered with a friendly smile and a slightly raised voice.

She peered across the table at me with narrowed eyes before returning her gaze to the screen before her.

Okay, the shy, quiet type.

I took a bite of my sandwich and then followed it with a swig of Coke as I contemplated my new table partner. Normally, I would have taken the hint, but her standoffishness annoyed me.

I love a good challenge.

Besides, if I had any chance of asking her about the lake episode, I'd have to gain her trust enough for her to talk to me.

I studied her at some length. She appeared particularly focused on whatever she was reading, and after a moment, I realized that she was using a Kindle.

Was she a nerdy bookworm or just the intellectual type?

Colbie Caillat's "Realize" played over the speaker system.

"You know, the music's not bad in here," I said.

She arched one eyebrow at me while removing an ear bud with one hand and holding her Kindle with the other.

"You're not going to let me be, are you?" she asked.

I innocently shrugged, letting her question go unanswered.

Instead, I asked, "Are you from Custer, oh-nameless-one?"

She cast a disparaging look at me.

"Gwen. And unlike you, I don't live in town."

I frowned.

"How did you know that I live here?"

She stared at me like I was the village idiot.

"It's a small town. Word gets around a place like Custer when somebody new moves here," she replied.

"Thanks for noticing," I said, and took another bite of my sandwich.

She returned to reading her Kindle, but lay her ear buds on the table before her.

"Don't flatter yourself," she said. "Your names and a family photo were in the town's e-newsletter that was spammed out to practically everyone in the county over a week ago."

"Just the same," I cheerfully said, though more to annoy her than anything else.

I began to wonder if, instead of being a nerd, Gwen was like so many other beautiful girls who I had met in the past; self-centered, unless you were on their radar.

Major disappointment.

I looked around, noting a tableful of girls casting glances at us and then trading hushed comments. An older couple drinking coffee at the table next to us also glanced in our direction before averting their gaze.

Weird.

"So, you like Kindle instead of Nook?" I asked in another attempt at small talk.

"Obviously, Sherlock," she replied shortly.

"Do you mean that in a Robert Downey, Jr. sort of way?"

She flatly ignored my snappy retort.

I paused to consider my next move.

"Whatcha' readin'?" I asked.

She sighed with a degree of exasperation.

"I *was* reading *Catching Fire* by Suzanne Collins," she

replied.

"Never heard of it," I said. "Any good?"

She shook her head slightly. "You've never heard of the *Hunger Games*? And yeah, it's good."

Okay, so maybe I *had* heard of that, after all.

"It's not really my thing," I said.

"Let me guess," she said. "You're not the 'reading type.'"

I tried not to smirk.

"Sure, I like to read," I said.

"I'll bet. Name the last book that you read," she challenged. "And *comics* don't count."

"Eww, sucker punch," I retorted in mock surprise. "First of all, graphic novels are cool. Alan Moore's stuff is wicked, and Neil Gaiman is the hands-down king. And second, I've been kind of preoccupied with moving the past couple of months. However, I last read one of Simon R. Green's *Nightside* novels. I think it was *Nightengale's Lament*."

She seemed somewhat surprised by my response.

"I haven't read anything by Simon Green," she admitted. "What genre does he write in?"

"Urban fantasy," I replied confidently before taking a bite of sandwich.

Score one for Mom having encouraged my reading as a kid.

"Hmm," she said, her brow arched in contemplation as she looked back down at her reader. "I figured you for football and comics. And maybe *porn*."

I flashed a sneer in her direction as she glowered back at me.

"Football, weightlifting, fishing, and occasionally reading," I rattled off in quick succession.

"Hmm," she said. "I also figured you for a jock," she added matter-of-factly.

Gwen returned to her Kindle, remaining silent.

"Look, I'm not just some jock," I said defensively. "I just happen to like football, and I worked really hard to get a starting spot on my old team."

Then I focused my attention upon my coveted dessert.

"Um, you do realize that Custer's football team has had two back-to-back losing seasons?" she asked, watching me dig into the piece of chocolate pie before me.

I looked up with a sour expression as I finished chewing what *had been* a great mouthful of pie.

"Yeah, I heard," I grumbled.

It was disappointing, to say the least. My former team had worked hard for a number of years and we'd been two games from the state championship last year. Now it felt like starting from scratch here in Custer.

Gwen adopted a sardonic grin and looked back down at her Kindle screen.

Despite Custer's recent football shortcomings, I was really looking forward to the prospect of playing football again, and I hoped that I'd have a chance to start at safety.

Instead of carrying on about all of that, I segued back to her again.

"*And?*" I asked expectantly. "C'mon, I shared my shortlist with you."

She glanced up at me with a slightly vexed expression. In truth, I found her expression to be sort of alluring.

Finally, she offered, "Fine. Poetry, reading, and day hiking. No fishing."

I nodded and looked around the dining room, gratefully noticing that most everyone's interest had returned to their own tables. The girls at the nearby table still peeked over at us, though. I looked back at Gwen, appreciating the way that her hair had partially fallen back around her face.

I decided to press my luck.

He who hesitates is lost.

"Hey, about the lake the other day," I began.

Gwen looked up at me with a guarded expression.

Suddenly, her phone vibrated on the tabletop. She swept it up with one hand and glanced at the screen.

"I have to go now," she abruptly insisted as she rose

from her chair and slipped a pair of sandals back onto her feet. "Nice chat," she shyly added as she quickly gathered up her Kindle and phone.

"Same here," I said. "I guess I'll see you at school on Monday."

Her expression darkened. "Don't count on it."

Before I could get up from of my seat, or ask her what she meant by that, she was already halfway to the door, and I could only watch as she walked away.

I certainly didn't mind the view, either.

As I sat back down, I couldn't help but notice that a number of people were staring at me again.

"Congratulations," said the old man sitting with his wife at the table next to mine.

"Thanks," I said.

Then I frowned.

"Why?" I asked.

"That's the most that Webber girl has talked to anyone in town in ages," he said.

"Oh," I muttered, somewhat baffled by that. I was still preoccupied with trying to figure out what Gwen had meant about not seeing her in school.

I knew then that I had to find out a lot more about Gwen Webber. And I still had yet to find out about the alligator that I'd seen.

Custer was growing more interesting by the minute.

CHAPTER 3

Monday rolled around quicker than I would have liked, but that might have just been my sense of avoidance concerning my newfound residency. Custer High School was on Wildcat Lane just down the street from the elementary school.

My first day went better than I expected. I felt pretty comfortable about my classes, and being able to take two of them online through Black Hills State University opened up time in my afternoon to attend an early football practice. I just had to make sure not to neglect my online studies, which meant setting aside precious time in the evenings after I got home.

I was able to meet with the football coach, Mr. Lambert, on my first day. Luckily for me, the team only had two players in the safety position, one of which was a walk-on sophomore who was playing his first year of football. Once Coach Lambert heard about my previous experience, he was happy to review my skills at a special practice after school that afternoon, and I was able to earn a nod to start at safety. That had definitely never happened to me before.

To say that I was stoked was an understatement.

I got to meet and spend time working out with the other players on the team, as well. By the time I made it home that evening, I was tired, but I felt really psyched. I was optimistic that maybe some things about living in Custer wouldn't be as bad as I feared.

However, not everything about that first day had been positive. I didn't happen to see Gwen Webber at school, and I'd kept a sharp lookout for her. Even if she hadn't been in any of my classes, I failed to see her during lunch, either. Her parting words to me on Sunday about not counting on seeing her at school replayed in my mind.

Was she attending another school?

That wasn't impossible, I supposed. But it was a pretty long commute to and from any surrounding towns just to attend school. She didn't look old enough to be a college student, but perhaps I'd been mistaken about that.

After relenting to my parents' badgering on filling them in on my day's events, I took a hot shower and settled in on the computer in my bedroom to log into my online courses.

My geometry class seemed pretty straightforward. I'd taken advanced math courses back in Springfield, so I didn't feel that intimidated. I introduced myself in the online forum and finished the first lesson and subsequent practice problems without difficulty.

When I logged into my American Literature course, I introduced myself in the main forum, and was surprised to see that the latest introduction was a posting from none other than Gwendolyn Webber!

It read, *"I'm Gwen Webber. My favorite genre is YA, but I like traditional literature, as well. Glad to be part of the group."*

I suddenly realized that I was sitting there grinning like an idiot. I quickly focused on formulating my introduction, which I revised four times before finally posting, *I'm Scott Blackstone. I like to read urban fantasy. I look forward to the semester.*

But as soon as I posted it, I started second-guessing my posting.

Lame. What the hell was wrong with me?

Geez, it was just an introduction. I bet that nobody probably even read them besides the instructor, anyway.

I proceeded into the first lesson, which was a brief recount of the history of American Literature dating back to the colonial period in the early 1600s. In addition, the class was supposed to read Nathaniel Hawthorne's *The Scarlet Letter* and prepare a report within two weeks.

I quickly decided that, of all of my classes, this was going to be the hardest.

After downloading an eBook copy of the novel for my Nook reader, I began reading, only to fall asleep sometime during the second chapter.

* * *

By the end of the week, I had firmly determined three things about my junior year of high school. First, I was probably going to enjoy playing football as a Wildcat, no matter how abbreviated the season turned out to be. I was able to impress a number of my teammates, and I got along well with pretty much everybody, including Coach Lambert.

Heck, it felt great just to be out on the field again.

Second, even though I missed my friends back in Springfield, I felt confident that I was going to be able to make new friends in Custer. Already, I had hit it off with the other starting safety on the team. Ben Collins was a senior, and he was quick to work with me on the defensive formations. Best of all, he shared my interest in both fishing and video games.

Third, I was going to have to work a lot harder if I expected to have any success getting to know Gwen. My efforts that first week to message her in our literature course had been nearly fruitless. Other than politely answering a question about how to interpret a short essay assignment, she wouldn't respond to any of my non-class-related questions. Not that I persisted overly hard at that; I didn't want to make it onto the instructor's troublemaker list.

During a break at football practice, I asked some of my teammates if they knew what classes Gwen was enrolled in at

Custer High. At first, the guys just cast knowing looks at each other.

"How'd you run into her?" asked Sutton, one of the linebackers. "She doesn't talk to hardly anybody, as far as I've noticed."

Finally, Valdez, another linebacker, said, "Too bad for you; she's *educación en casa.*"

I frowned at him.

"What?"

Valdez chuckled. "Home-schooled."

I nodded.

"Oh. Why?" I asked.

My fellow safety, Ben Collins, clasped me on the shoulder and suggested, "Leave that one alone, Blackstone. You just got here, so why not take your time and look around."

"The girl's damaged goods, man," said Benedict, the sophomore cornerback. "You're better off checking out some of the girls here at our school."

"Or there's quite a few cute girls in Hill City," offered Dobbs, a junior lineman.

"What? There's exactly three cute girls in Hill City, loser," chided VanHorn, a senior linebacker.

Nobody else was willing to say much else about Gwen. However, rather than deter me, it only heightened my curiosity about her.

During the day, though primarily due to football practice and getting established in my classes, it had been relatively easy not to obsess over Gwen. However, each evening, she frequently returned to the forefront of my thoughts.

On more than one occasion I wondered, *Why her?*

Maybe it was partly due to how attractive she was. Of course, the air of mystery that she maintained certainly kept my attention. Then there was the sarcastic wit that she had displayed during our brief at the bakery café.

I couldn't help but smile over that.

Okay, no matter the reasons, she's definitely captured my interest.

In the end, maybe I'd find that Gwen wasn't all that interesting or appealing. I'd known girls back in Springfield who had looked attractive or seemed interesting, but later turned out to be conceited or annoying.

However, I'd have to get to know Gwen better before I came to any of those prospective conclusions.

I realized that what I needed was a plan of action.

But first, I had to eat. It was Friday evening, and I'd agreed to meet some of my teammates at the Pizza Palace in town. As I rushed downstairs with keys in hand, I heard my parents' voices in the kitchen.

"Going to the pizza place," I said as I hastily peered into the kitchen. "Be back later."

"Hey, take two seconds and congratulate your mother," Dad insisted.

I paused just long enough to say, "Congrats, Mom!"

Mom folded her arms before her and Dad gave me the evil eye.

Pausing another moment longer, I asked, "Okay, sorry. What's the good news, Mom?"

"Today, I got a position as a nurse at the Custer Regional Hospital over on Montgomery Street," she proudly announced. "A spot opened up when one of the nurses left for a position at one of the hospitals in Rapid City."

"That's great, Mom," I said, enveloping her in a big hug.

"We've invited her new boss, Dr. Webber, over for dinner tomorrow night, in fact," Dad said.

My eyes immediately targeted my father.

"Did you say *Webber*?" I asked.

"Olivia Webber," Mom confirmed. "I invited her and her daughter, Gwendolyn, over. I thought it would be a sociable way to get to know my new boss."

Fate could definitely be interesting, I considered.

"Really?" I asked. "That's pretty cool."

Mom frowned.

"It is?"

"Wonders never cease," Dad muttered. "Our son's

finally embracing social graces. Maybe soon, he'll remember to take the trash out on Fridays."

I shook my head at him.

"Thanks, Dad," I said.

"So, don't make any plans," Mom instructed. "We're having grilled steaks and potatoes."

The prospects were definitely interesting. Of course, Gwen, or no Gwen, I wasn't passing up a grilled steak with potato, either.

"You got it," I said as I barreled to the front door with a newfound reason to celebrate over pizza.

CHAPTER 4

By late Saturday afternoon, I'd finished some homework, including reading more of *The Scarlet Letter*. I prepared the charcoal grill that my dad had picked up at the local camping supplies dealer.

"I thought you ordered a propane grill from Rapid City?" I asked him.

"They're on backorder," he lamented as he liberally applied lighting fluid to the coals.

As the match caught against the fumes, the grill lit up in a sudden burst of flame. I jerked Dad's arm to pull him off to one side before the flames caught his shirt.

"Damn!" he exclaimed with a wide-eyed expression.

"We almost needed the doctor early," I said, grateful that my reflexes were quick.

"Yeah," he muttered. "Thanks, son; and let's not mention this to your mother. Hey, keep an eye on this while I check on the steak preparations."

I grinned as he disappeared into the house.

A half hour later, the doorbell rang as I finished buttoning one of my dressier shirts and checked myself in the mirror. I shot downstairs to the front door while tucking my shirt into my jeans.

"I've got it," I called to my parents.

As I swept the door open, a beautiful lady stood before me. She was like a taller version of Gwen, only older and with auburn hair and hazel eyes.

"Hello, Dr. Webber," I politely offered, though my eyes searched past her, looking for Gwen. "I'm Scott. Please, come in."

Her bright smile made her face light up as she entered. "Thank you, Scott."

Dr. Webber entered, revealing no sight of Gwen as I noted the black Cadillac Escalade parked in our driveway.

Where was Gwen?

I closed the door and turned around to watch Dr. Webber with a perplexed expression as she was introduced to my dad.

"We're so happy that you could make it, Dr. Webber," Mom offered.

"Please, outside of the office it's just Olivia," she insisted. "And I must apologize on behalf of my daughter. Gwen's working on some important school deadlines so she couldn't accompany me this evening."

"We understand," Mom replied as her eyes caught mine. "Perhaps another time, then. May I get you something to drink? I just finished brewing some iced tea for us, but I also made some chilled lemonade."

"Tea sounds nice, thanks," Dr. Webber replied as the she and my parents made their way into the kitchen.

Just great. This evening is going to be a blast, I thought dejectedly.

I half-heartedly went out to the patio to check the grill, but I was suddenly less interested in the steaks that awaited us that evening.

Eating my dinner in relative silence, I briefly answered some of Dr. Webber's questions about my interests, including, at the behest of my dad, a brief commentary about our prospects for the upcoming football season.

Dr. Webber seemed really nice; there was something that felt very comforting about her, but I couldn't place my finger on it.

Then the conversation turned back to Mom and Dad, and I fell silent as I ate my meal. I was very disappointed that Gwen hadn't accompanied her mom, and I couldn't help but wonder if the reason was something other than homework. *Me, for instance.*

As I absently listened, Dr. Webber described how she had relocated to Custer just after Gwen had been born. She had accepted an offer from the town to be the primary care physician at the Custer Regional Hospital just after she finished medical school. She loved small towns, and was originally from Lakeville, Minnesota, just south of Minneapolis.

However, she earned my rapt attention as she touchingly described how she was a widow, including how her husband, Frank, and her son, Tom, had died in a horrible car accident five years prior on Interstate 385, just north of town.

I momentarily wondered if that had something to do with why Gwen was so shy and standoffish.

"I'm so sorry," Mom offered.

"That's just terrible," Dad said.

"Thank you," Dr. Webber replied. "The town has been so supportive since then. This really is a wonderful place to live."

The conversation turned less interesting to me as my parents alternated the recitation about our family, Dad's own town roots, and what had brought us to relocate to Custer.

After dinner, we relocated to the patio, where the three of them sipped wine and visited at length. I nursed a Coca-Cola, slightly jealous of them, though my thoughts were still mulling over what Dr. Webber had told us during dinner.

As I slipped into the kitchen to put my empty soda can into the recycling bin, Mom entered behind me to refill her glass with wine.

"Scott, if you'd like to slip away it would be perfectly fine," she offered. "I'm sure that you're probably bored listening to us old people talk."

Smirking, I gave her a quick peck on her cheek.

"You'll never be old, Mom," I quipped. "And thanks. I'll probably take a walk around town."

I was grateful to be excused and went upstairs to hang my briefly-worn dress shirt back on its hanger in the closet. Then I went for a walk.

* * *

Saturday night in Custer was sedate, to say the least. Traffic down Custer Street was relatively light; a mix of locals and some visitors who were frequenting the town's restaurants. I momentarily considered that if I wanted a part-time job, I might end up working in one of them. Most were service-oriented as the town's businesses catered to jobs surrounding the tourist industry.

Not exactly a lot of exciting career opportunities, I mused.

I walked past the darkened windows of Betty's Bakery & Café, wishing that they were open so I could have something for dessert. I crossed to the north side of the street and made my way eastward toward the Java World Coffee Shop. I recalled that it was open until relatively late and I thought that they stocked dessert items.

It was somewhat surprising to find the shop relatively empty for just past eight o'clock. I waved to the cute blonde-haired girl behind the counter, who I recognized from school but couldn't remember her name. Then my eyes fell upon someone seated in the back of the room with her back to the wall reading a Kindle.

Gwen Webber.

"How's it going?" the girl behind the counter asked.

"Just great," I half-heartedly replied.

Gwen looked up and our eyes met for a split second, just long enough for me to see the slightly surprised look on her face quickly turn sour.

I broke eye contact with her and turned to leave as a simple, stark realization flashed through my mind.

Gwen wasn't at all interested in socializing with either me or my family.

I felt as if I'd been such a loser to be so interested in her. I shook my head in frustration, briskly walking westward down the sidewalk back from where I came.

The door to the coffee shop flew open behind me, and I heard Gwen yell, "Scott!"

I didn't turn around and instead kept walking.

"Please, wait," I heard her say.

The sound of pursuing footsteps caused me to slow as I heaved a heavy sigh.

What now?

I looked back over my shoulder to see her standing on the sidewalk with a helpless expression on her face.

"I'm sorry," she said in quiet voice.

"Don't worry about it," I replied tightly. "I won't bother you anymore."

"You're not bothering me," she meekly said.

I frowned and turned to see her looking at me with a helpless expression.

What the hell?

"What?" I asked.

"Give me chance to explain," she said with a slightly pleading expression in her eyes.

"Why?" I asked.

What I really wanted to know was why she suddenly cared what I thought about her. She had seemed relatively unconcerned just the other day.

She started to reply but hesitated.

"I feel kind of ashamed, and I don't want you to hate me over what happened tonight."

"Because I matter all of the sudden?" I pressed.

One side of her mouth upturned slightly.

"I dunno. You seem like a nice enough kind of guy," she said with a shrug. "Just come back inside and hear me out."

I stared at her, wondering whether or not to join her.

"Why not," I replied, walking back toward the coffee

shop alongside her.

However strange, it's a start, I silently considered.

As I sat opposite Gwen at the table where she'd been sitting, I took a swig from my glass of raspberry-flavored iced tea as Sea Wolf's "You're a Wolf" played over the shop's overhead speakers.

It was a little hard to believe that after what seemed like prolonged efforts and waiting, I was once again sitting across a table from the elusive *Gwen Webber*, and at her invitation, no less.

That's not to say that I wasn't still annoyed with her over her no-show at dinner.

She gazed down into her Styrofoam drink cup as if it was an oracle or something, and I wondered if she was going to lose her nerve and just sit quietly.

Finally, she said, "Please understand, I usually don't spend a lot of time around people. They make me nervous."

"Is that why you didn't come over to my house with your mom tonight?" I asked.

Gwen nodded, looking up from her drink to meet my eyes.

"Why do people make you feel nervous? Does it have something to do with your father and brother?"

She frowned at me.

"Your mom mentioned the accident this evening," I said. "She seems really nice, by the way."

"Yeah, she's pretty awesome, actually," she agreed. "And yes, the accident has something to do with how things are with me."

I tried to make sense of what little she was telling me.

"I'm sorry about your brother and dad," I offered. "I can't imagine going through that."

She looked up at me with a tender expression.

"You don't know the half---" she started to say. Then she stopped and frowned.

"Listen, Scott. I really appreciate you wanting to get to know me and everything," she began. "I just don't want to mislead you into thinking that there's a future with us."

"Future?" I asked incredulously. "There's not even a *present* between us yet. I just want to get to know you. I mean, I hardly know *anybody* in this town. I'm practically still a stranger here."

"Yeah, well…me, too," she added. "And I've lived her for most of my life."

All right, that caught me off guard.

"Okay, I'm not even sure what that means," I said.

"Look, it's complicated and not something that I want to go into right now," she said. "I really just wanted to tell you that I wasn't trying to be rude to you or your family tonight. It's all me; I'm the problem, not you. And if it makes you feel any better, you seem really nice, and I enjoyed our chat the other day."

Ouch. Lukewarm feelings were worse than negative ones when it came to the opposite sex.

"I think that I'm more than just nice," I said confidently.

She glanced at her watch.

"That's probably true," she hedged as she got up from her seat. "Listen, I have to get back before Mom gets home. I convinced her that I was staying home to do homework, so could we keep this meeting just between us?"

"Oh, sure," I said with a degree of exasperation, rising to follow her from the coffee shop.

The girl at the counter watched us intently as we passed by her on the way to the door.

"Take care," the girl suggested which caused me to look back at her.

The girl's eyes widened and she focused a purposeful stare upon Gwen as she walked through the door in front of me.

Frowning back at her in confusion, I followed Gwen outside.

"I'm really sorry about tonight, Scott," Gwen said as she went around to the side of the coffee shop and stopped dead in her tracks.

I looked at the older model two-door Suzuki Sidekick parked before her. It was gray with a pink stripe down the side, and its windshield was covered with the message 'Stay Home Ghost Girl' written in what looked like white shoe polish.

"Dammit," she cursed.

I scanned the area and noticed a trio of teenage girls heading up the street away from us, laughing and giggling as they ran. As they passed underneath a streetlight, I thought that I recognized one of the girls from school.

"Uh, I'll get some paper towels from the shop," I offered.

But Gwen pulled her keys from her pocket, insisting, "No, it's fine. I'll wash it off at home."

"Hey, that stuff is kind of blocking your view," I said, walking after her. "It's dark out, after all."

"I'm close; I live just a few miles north of town," she argued.

I growled over her stubbornness, pulled my T-shirt off, and used it to wipe the driver's side of the windshield clean for her. The polish wiped off relatively easily.

"There," I said resolutely, looking back at her. "See? That wasn't so hard, now was it?"

I noticed that she was staring at my bare chest while biting her bottom lip.

"Nice," she muttered.

I grinned.

Gwen quickly averted her gaze from me and stammered, "I mean, it's all good. The, um, windshield."

She shook her head in apparent frustration and hastily unlocked her SUV.

I held the driver's side door open for her.

"Thanks," she tentatively offered with a quick glance at me.

"Anytime," I replied. "Be safe," I added.

Be safe?

I stifled a groan over how lame that just sounded.

She nodded and gave me a cute little wave before turning onto the main street heading west.

I was amused to no end over her initial reaction and I thoroughly enjoyed my walk home in the cool evening air.

After I finished showering later that night, I flexed my biceps, deltoids, and traps while observing my image with satisfaction in the bathroom mirror and recalled Gwen's reaction earlier that evening. It turned out that all those hours of weightlifting were well worth the time spent.

I popped my ear buds in and listened to music on my iPod as I checked my email and Facebook for messages. To my pleasant surprise, I had a new Facebook friendship request from Gwen.

She also sent me a direct message that said, '*Thanks for the help tonight, Scott. You are definitely more than just nice.*'

I smiled as I clicked *Accept.*

CHAPTER 5

By Monday, word had quickly circulated about my meeting with Gwen on Saturday night. I suspected that it must have been the girl at the counter who'd spread the word. It amazed me that no one had anything more interesting to talk about.

As I walked through the hallway on the way to third period, I caught a glimpse of one of the girls, a redhead, who had been part of the group running away from the scene of the prank against Gwen. She was talking with some friends at her locker.

I half-considered walking past them, but then stopped at the last minute to confront her.

"Hey, that was pretty crappy what you did to Gwen's SUV Saturday night," I said.

The girl looked up at me with surprise and her friends fell silent as they stared at me.

"Yeah, whatever. No harm done and nobody got hurt," she said. "And who are you supposed to be, hero? Her boyfriend maybe?"

I gritted my teeth.

"Just a friend," I said. "For now."

"Well, you should get your freak on with someone less freaky," suggested a blonde-haired girl standing beside the redhead.

"I don't much care for bullies," I said emphatically. "Gwen didn't do anything to any of you, as far as I know."

They just stared at me and the blonde-haired girl rolled her eyes.

"And why did you call her ghost girl?" I demanded.

The girls exchanged glances, and the redhead replied, "Because, it's like she's there, but she's still invisible to everybody. She haunts this town, just hanging around but never talking to anyone."

Instead of wasting my time with further useless chatter, I turned and walked away. Before I made it ten feet, a girl with short black hair and Goth-like eyeliner motioned to me with a slight jerk of her head. She casually leaned back against her locker clutching her books close to her chest.

"Yeah?" I asked suspiciously.

"I heard what you said to Tammy over there," she said. "That was nice to stand up for Gwen. Very few people do nowadays."

"Are you friends with Gwen?" I asked.

She shrugged. "We used to be."

"Yeah, well, Gwen seems like she could use a few friends nowadays," I observed.

"She had quite a few friends when she was still going to the Middle School."

"So, you didn't stay in touch when she started being home-schooled?" I asked.

"Hey, that wasn't my choice," she replied. "Gwen cut *me* off years ago. She withdrew from everyone, in fact."

"Why?"

"Dunno. I guess we just slowly drifted apart."

I considered that.

"I'm Amy, by the way," she offered.

"Nice to meet you," I said. "I'm Scott."

She rolled her eyes at me.

"Oh my *Goth*, Mr. Clueless," she said. "Everyone knows *you*. Check ya' later."

Then she hastily darted down the hallway in the opposite direction, and I couldn't help but chuckle as I headed to Personal Finance.

* * *

I spent the remainder of the week completely bogged down with homework, including preparing for a geometry test for my online class. And I still had to write the report on *The Scarlet Letter*. Fortunately, Gwen had been kind enough to offer her own insights on the assignment, and it gave me some ideas on how I could approach my report.

However, what I wanted to ask her about was the alligator that I'd seen at the lake. Maybe once I felt more comfortable with our newfound friendship, I'd be sure to ask about that.

But, alligators aside, the anticipated highlight event of my week was our first football game of the season coming up on Friday, including my debut starting at safety. We were scheduled to play against the More Cavaliers, one of Custer's biggest rivals, and a team that had won the matchup repeatedly in recent years.

At least, it was a home game for us.

Mom and Dad were also excited for me, and the days flew by in no time at all. By Friday, the entire school had a vibe about it that it was palpable. I started getting a case of nerves about two hours prior to game time.

As I suited up in my uniform, I glanced around the locker room at my teammates. The purple and gold seemed like foreign colors to me. Everyone appeared to be feeling the same nervous energy in the room, and more than one person had to throw up prior to our march out to take the field. Coach Lambert led us in a team prayer and challenged us to stay focused and execute our game plan.

I felt more than ready to prove myself.

On the sidelines after we took the field, I scanned the bleachers, which were packed with people either wearing our colors or More's royal blue and white. The cheerleaders shouted out to the crowd as our band hammered out our school song. I kept scanning our side of the field and spotted Mom and Dad sitting in the stands. Finally, I saw Gwen's mother sitting off to one side of the second from the top row.

I waved at Dr. Webber and she waved back at me.

However, to my disappointment, there was no sign of Gwen.

The kickoff sounded like a thunderclap, and our defense took the field first. On More's first drive, they marched all the way down to our twenty-two yard line. Then, I was tested by a powerful pass to a receiver in my zone on third down. I barely managed to tip the ball at the last minute, holding them to a field goal.

Ben Collins high-fived me for my effort.

By half-time, the score was thirteen to ten; we were only trailing by three points. Coach Lambert directed us in some corrections to our game plan, and we raced back out to the field for the second half.

Our offense played hard and managed to match More on scoring, including two additional touchdowns. However, More mirrored us, and we still trailed by three points for the third quarter and most of the fourth. To my credit, I did a pretty good job covering receivers and even assisted with a number of tackles.

It felt great to be playing football again.

With only two minutes left in the game, More managed to drive the ball down to our three-yard line. We were pretty winded on defense, and a third down fake pass enabled the Cavalier's running back to sneak into the end zone. However, we blocked the extra point, bringing our deficit to nine points.

We needed two scores with less than two minutes left in the game.

Our offense worked hard to get us into field goal range with the game's final seconds ticking down. Our kicker, Zack

Anderson, managed an eighteen-yard field goal by the width of the football, but we'd run out of time. We lost the game by six points.

While disappointing, we'd fought hard during the game. At least the Coach said that we did a better job against More than had been done in the previous three matchups with them. Although he didn't go into a lot of details, Coach pointed out that we had to make a number of improvements.

"I've gotta work harder on my tight coverage skills," I muttered.

"Don't worry, Blackstone," Ben assured me. "We're gonna' hone those skills of yours. You'll be ready for the next game."

We were scheduled to go to Hot Springs to play the Bison team the following Friday. I vowed to work extra hard so that I wouldn't make the same mistakes twice.

By the time I'd showered and changed into my jeans and a clean jersey, most of the crowd had dispersed. However, Dr. Webber and my parents were standing near the concession stand waiting for me.

"Nice job, son," Dad proudly declared. "You've improved a lot since you played last year."

Mom added that she noticed I was doing a better job tackling.

I thanked them, though I still felt bad that we had lost. I felt certain that if we'd only had another five minutes, we could have tied up the game.

"Want to grab something to eat, Scott? I know I do," Dad said. "Games always make me hungry."

"Hungry? You had nachos and two Cokes during the game, Bob," Mom admonished.

"Hey, that was just an appetizer," he replied defensively.

"It's a good thing that we own a grocery store now," Mom said to Dr. Webber, who grinned.

"Actually, I think that I'll pick up something to take home for Gwen and me," Dr. Webber said. "But you played a great game, Scott, and I'm sure things will improve as the season progresses. I can tell that both our offense and defense has a lot of talent this year."

We said goodbye, and I asked her to say hello to Gwen for me. Then, Mom, Dad, and I dropped by Rushmore Burgers on Custer Street on the way home. The burgers and fries tasted great, but I still kept replaying the game over in my mind, wondering what else I could've done on defense.

Later that night, I traded Facebook messages with Gwen as "Gravity" by Hit the Lights played on my iPod.

Whatcha' doing this weekend?

Gwen replied, *Working on the essay for Lit.*

I texted, *Want to meet for dinner Sat nt? We can proof essays.*

In truth, I hadn't even started on the essay yet.

She replied, *We could email r essays.*

I paused.

Easier to talk in person. We have to eat sometime, right?

A few minutes passed with no response, and I wondered if she'd abandoned our chat.

Finally, she replied: *Ok. Pizza?*

I fist-pumped into empty air a few times in victory.

I sent, *Yeah, sounds fine. Pizza Palace at 7pm?*

Gwen replied: *Ok. See you then.*

"Oh-yeah!" I said.

Though only a date, at least I won *something* tonight.

Then I realized that I had an entire essay to write by Saturday evening.

"Okay, that's just craptastic," I groaned.

I headed downstairs to retrieve some Red Bulls from the fridge. It was going to be a long night.

CHAPTER 6

I spent most of Friday night and much of early Saturday in a mad race to both start and finish my essay. At least, I'd actually read *The Scarlet Letter,* so that I had an idea of what I was talking about.

I did some weightlifting that afternoon to work off some of the tension from my essay, and then showered and changed into clothes that were my best look—jeans and a black T-shirt. I almost forgot to grab my assignment from off of the printer before I left.

Just before seven o'clock, I walked into Pizza Palace with essay in hand. Honestly, it felt weird carrying around a literature essay on a Saturday night. In fact, it felt kind of nerdy, so I folded it in half.

Jessie J's "Domino" played as I scanned the busy dining room. I quickly spotted Gwen sitting in a corner booth with one side of her hair partly blocking her face.

"Hey, there's our next college draft safety!" boomed Ben from a nearby booth.

I looked up at Ben and noticed that he was sitting with his girlfriend, Carolyn. One of our defensive linemen, VanHorn, and his girlfriend were also sitting at the table.

Reaching out to meet Ben's hand in a quick fraternal slap, I quipped, "What're you troublemakers doin' out tonight?"

VanHorn nodded at me and replied, "Just ordered a pizza, and then we're headed to a movie. Wanna' join us? Always room for one more."

"Nah, thanks, man," I said. "I'm meeting someone."

I glanced over to where Gwen sat, and found her intently staring at me.

"Catch you guys later, and have fun at the movie," I said with a quick wave.

As I approached Gwen, she looked up with a wry expression.

"Hi," I said, slipping into the booth seat across from her.

"Well, well, if it isn't Mr. Popularity himself," she teased.

"C'mon, now," I said.

"We can always cancel if you'd rather hang out with your friends," she offered.

"Are you just tryin' to get rid of me?" I replied.

She regarded me with a wary look in her eyes.

I stared directly at her and said, "Listen, I can't think of anyone I'd rather be with tonight."

Her eyes widened and she broke eye contact to look down at the tabletop.

"Cool," she said nonchalantly.

"What can I get you two to drink?" asked the waitress, who suddenly appeared at our booth side.

"Coke for me," I said.

"Same, thanks," Gwen said.

"I'll be right back to take your order," the waitress said, though I caught her curious look at Gwen before she turned around.

I scanned the menu for a few seconds.

"So then, pizza?" I prompted, once again focused on the attractive person sitting opposite me.

"We *are* at a pizza place, after all," she said.

I studied her with an overly dramatic arch of one eyebrow.

"Yeah, but I'd swear you were just giving off a calzone

vibe a minute ago," I teased.

She adopted a mock-imperious expression.

"I think not," she said in a nasally tone. "Name your pizza and prepare to be judged."

"Combo with all the meats," I insisted. "Hold the anchovies."

She wrinkled her nose. "Ugh, way too heavy."

I shook my head.

"Naturally. All right, you name it, then," I challenged.

"Pepperoni," she blurted before adding, "No, make that *double* pepperoni with black olives."

"Acceptable enough," I declared.

We ordered a large version of her preferred style of pizza, complete with the salad bar.

"Missed you at the game last night," I said as I dug into my salad.

"Not my thing, really," she replied offhandedly.

I frowned.

"Your mom was there," I said.

"Mom goes to all of the games," she replied. "She likes watching, and she volunteers to be an attending physician in case there's an injury."

I nodded.

"You could've watched me play," I pressed.

She shrugged, picking at her salad.

"Maybe some other time," she said.

"Sure," I replied, somewhat doubting her sincerity.

She looked up at me with a penetrating expression and then diverted her gaze to the surrounding dining room.

"What did you do today?" I asked.

"Spent some time in the forest near our house," she replied.

"I see. And how were the Keebler Elves today?" I asked with a straight face.

She gave me a bland look.

"Very funny, muscle boy," she said.

"Thanks for noticing, actually," I said while flexing my

left bicep. "I did hit the weights for a little workout this afternoon, as a matter of fact."

Her eyes gravitated to my arm and then lingered on me before she looked away again.

"Not bad," she said, though I thought that her face looked a little flushed for a moment.

I grinned.

She shyly smiled back.

"Well, since you asked, this afternoon I went back over my *Scarlet Letter* essay one last time. Oh, and I even watched the movie from back in the nineties starring Demi Moore," she added. "Although, it really wasn't done the same way as the book."

"Demi who?" I asked.

She rolled her eyes at me.

"Never mind," she said. "So, are you going to let me read your essay, or what?"

I searched the area around me, belatedly realizing that I had absently placed my slightly wrinkled, stapled effort on the seat next to me. I pushed it across the table toward her. In exchange, and with a flourish of her hand as she picked mine up from before her, she offered me her essay, neatly enveloped in a red plastic folder.

It looked professional, to say the least.

"Nice, but we're just supposed to upload the electronic file, aren't we?" I asked with raised brows.

She shrugged.

"I impressed you, at least," she replied with a smug expression.

I scowled at her and started reading her essay. What I quickly discovered was that Gwen had a real talent for writing, which put my own abilities to shame. Her writing style was both insightful and reflective.

She had been really thorough in her analysis of the book, and I realized that she was way out of my league on the subject.

I suddenly hoped that the rest of the class didn't turn in

essays as good as Gwen's, or I might get less than a passing grade.

Our pizza arrived soon after I finished reading her essay.

Setting it aside, I offered, "Wow, you did a great job."

Then I noticed that she'd procured an ink pen and was marking up my essay. In fact, not a page went untouched.

I ate a slice of pizza while pensively watching her.

Finally, she flipped my essay closed and pushed it back across the table at me.

"Not bad," she said. "I offered some comments and corrections that you might want to make; just to help polish it up, of course."

"Oh, thanks," I replied as she reached for a slice of pizza.

We ate in relative silence for a few minutes as I thought about how smart, as well as how physically attractive, she was. Both were in stark contrast to her general personality, which seemed not only awkward, but socially uncomfortable and somewhat standoffish.

What caused a person to be such a blend of contrasts?

"You sure got quiet all of a sudden," she observed.

"Just thinking," I said.

"About what?"

"You," I said.

"Yeah?" she asked, sounding suddenly wary. "Like what?"

"Thinking about how pretty and smart you are," I replied.

She appeared uncertain how to respond to that and quickly took a bite of pizza.

"And thinking that I'd like to go out with you," I added.

She stopped chewing and stared at me.

"Well?"

"Well, what?" she asked.

"Will you go out with me?"

"Uh, we are out," she said.

"No, I mean on a *real* date," I clarified.

She upended her glass of Coke and emptied the contents in a few swallows.

I waited, but when she sat her glass down, she remained silent.

"Well?" I asked.

She stared at me.

"I really don't think that's a good idea, Scott," she said emphatically.

"What, do you turn into a werewolf at sundown or something?" I teased.

"You don't---" she began.

"Unless you aren't interested in me, at which point---" I interrupted.

"No, that's not it," she cut me off.

I frowned.

"Then, why not?" I insisted.

She sighed and gazed up at the ceiling as if expecting to find the words that she needed.

"Just how badly do you think that you want a date with me?" she pressed.

I blinked and stared back at her.

"I'm not easily deterred when I have my mind set on something," I replied. "Or someone," I added.

Okay, that might have sounded a little stalker-ish, in retrospect.

She leveled her blue-eyed gaze upon me, which seemed suddenly hard.

"Listen, what I meant---" I began.

"Fine," she interrupted. "I'll consider going out with you. Of course, that's *if* you make an interception during next Friday's game."

I just stared at her as if she had lost her mind. We were scheduled to play the Hot Springs Bison's, and according to Ben, they had a tough offense that rarely turned over the ball.

"So, you're not going to tell me why I shouldn't go out with you," I observed. "Instead, you're going to issue a challenge to me?"

Gwen shrugged.

"That's my condition. Take it or leave it," she said.

I half-considered getting up from the table without even saying goodnight or goodbye. It was becoming apparent to me that she harbored a number of issues that made it more than difficult to get to know her. It was little wonder that people in town had trouble interacting with her.

"Okay," I said, undeterred. "We'll just see how the game goes on Friday, then."

Her eyes widened with surprise.

"Anyway, thanks for the help with my essay. This has been such a *blast*, and I hope that the rest of your weekend is epic," I said, picking up both the check and my inked-up essay.

"So, now you're angry?" she accused.

"Me, angry? Nah, I'm just great," I said.

Then I turned and made my way through the dining room toward the cash register near the parlor's entrance.

What sort of clown question is that? I mean, just how oblivious could she be?

I was absolutely pissed off over Gwen's persistent avoidance. It would have been so much easier just to forget her and start trying to date some of the other girls at school.

As I climbed into my SUV, I wondered if I could actually manage an interception next Friday. And if I did manage one, would I still care to collect on a date with Gwen?

By Monday morning, after vacillating between feelings of annoyance and confusion all day Sunday, I still hadn't arrived at an adequate answer to that question.

CHAPTER 7

The next week went by pretty quickly. Between the nearly embarrassing quantity of changes to my essay that Gwen had recommended and extended football practices after school, I'd been busy. Of course, I had also spent some time ruminating over Gwen's strange condition for earning a date with her, as well as her persistently standoffish behavior.

It's not as if Gwen had even mentioned the topic since Saturday night; quite the opposite, in fact. During the week, she messaged me about topics related to our online literature class a couple of times, almost as if our conversation had never happened.

I was beginning to wonder if she was seriously mental, or if perhaps she had some odd disease that messed with her brain.

There were moments that I merely felt angry, while other times, I felt determined in my resolve to meet or exceed her strange pre-date condition. Most of all, I couldn't figure out why Gwen couldn't manage to confide in me to explain why she felt the way that she did about having difficulties getting to know me, or anybody else for that matter.

For all I knew, her reasons might be absolutely valid. They could also be completely off-the-charts ridiculous.

Heck, it could be virtually anything. And frankly, nothing

would have surprised me.

On Wednesday, my endless contemplations got the better of me, and I wondered why I even bothered trying to get to know a girl who was seemingly content to remain so withdrawn. It wasn't as if there weren't other cute and intelligent girls at school who had caught my eye.

Granted, Gwen was definitely drop-dead gorgeous. She had looked great in the form-fitting shorts that she had on when I first talked to her that day in Betty's Bakery.

Upon further reflection, I realized that it was more than mere attraction that drew me to Gwen. She was interesting, and her unconventional personality was intriguing to me. Yet, there was an additional quality about Gwen, though I was hard-pressed to put it into words.

It was as if there was some internal spark that flared within me whenever I was around her. Was it chemistry, or something stronger?

I only knew that she evoked strong feelings inside of me that I hadn't felt with other girls. It felt unique and special, though given Gwen's continued evasiveness, somewhat infuriating.

She was driving me crazy in a number of ways; both desirable and perplexing.

Mom and Dad noticed that I seemed distracted during the week, and they lightly pressed me to talk about it a couple of times. But since they were both acquainted with Gwen's mother, I didn't feel comfortable talking with them about the matter.

Instead, I approached my friend, Ben, before practice on Wednesday. And given Gwen's notorious reputation among some of my peers, I cautiously steered us to a location that was safely out of earshot from the other players before I broached the topic.

"So, let me get this straight, Blackstone," he asked. "You have to make an interception this Friday just to *earn* the *chance* for a date with this girl?"

"Yeah, that's pretty much it," I replied.

He shook his head.

"You really like her, don't you?" he asked.

"Sure. I mean, I think so," I replied.

"But?" he asked.

"I don't know, man," I said. "Part of me feels like her little test, or whatever you want to call it, is just childish; like I'm being played or something. To be honest, it makes me feel kind of resentful, and I don't want to feel that way about her."

"Yeah, man, I can see that," he agreed. "Still, if you think Gwen's worth it, maybe you should go for it. Hey, it isn't as if we couldn't use a couple of good interceptions against the Bison team on Friday."

I chuckled.

"Too true. But can we just keep this between us for now?"

Ben nodded and said, "Yeah, sure, bro."

I picked up my helmet and we both headed toward the practice field.

"Good luck with that girl," Ben said.

A dose of good luck was exactly what I seemed to need.

* * *

Hot Springs was only a little over thirty miles from Custer, so the team's bus ride that Friday afternoon had been relatively short. Much to my surprise, a large number of Custer residents made the journey with us. A couple of my teammates assured me that a steady stream of fans would fill the stadium by the time that kick-off arrived.

The Bison's were one of Custer's big rivals, and their royal blue and white colors reminded me of the More Cavaliers, who we'd played the prior week. It felt as if our team was getting to have a 'replay' of last week's game; only this time, we were steadfastly determined to make an even better showing.

As we took to the field for pre-game stretches, I scanned

the stands to see if I could find my parents. After two sweeps, I spotted them on the third row. However, I didn't see anyone else who had made my internalized attendance list; specifically Gwen.

Not that I'd actually expected her to show up, of course; merely hopeful.

Coach Lambert was fired up almost as much as the players and he gave a fiery locker room speech. By game time, I felt adrenaline coupled with a case of pregame nerves coursing through my body, and I thought that I would explode if I had to wait another minute.

I was ready to prove myself; prove my worth.

My motivation wasn't so much just for Gwen and her ultimatum; though that was a small part of it. It was mainly to prove to myself that I deserved to start at safety; that I could help to put my team in a position to win. I owed that much to my team, as well as to myself.

We took the field amidst the shouts from a stadium filled with Custer fans that had made the drive to watch us; a combination of parents, teachers, and other town residents who, I was told, showed up at most games, home or away. The band was in rare form as it blared out our fight song.

We had the ball to start the game, but our offense was halted in its tracks, achieving only one first down. Following a muffed catch by one of the Bison's key receivers on punt return, the guy still managed to bring the ball out to their thirty-two yard line. I had to fight against one of their veteran receivers, Hunt, who was difficult to cover because he was always changing direction almost in mid-stride.

Despite Hunt's shrewd technique, I had to grudgingly admit that the guy was an accomplished receiver. He was so fast that my immediate concern was giving up a big play by missing a tackle and being outrun. My central focus was to keep him in front of me.

Halfway through the second quarter, Ben corralled me on the sideline to give me some quick tips. He'd noticed that Hunt had a habit of feigning to his right before cutting across to his left on receptions.

"You've gotta' react faster when you see him beat our cornerbacks," Ben urged. "Cut to his left sooner and you can disrupt his pattern better."

"Got it," I said. "Thanks!"

"Go get 'em, son!" My dad yelled from the stands behind me.

I turned to look at him, and that's when I saw Gwen and her mom sitting next to my parents. Gwen's and my eyes met for only a brief second before she quickly looked away.

I could scarcely believe that Gwen had come to the game, though I ventured that she just wanted to make sure that I didn't lie about any prospective interceptions.

Managing to secure a date with her was the least of my problems. Given the way that Hunt was playing, I was more worried about giving up a touchdown and letting my team down.

"Blackstone, get in there!" Coach Lambert yelled.

I popped my helmet back onto my head and ran out to my position.

Fortunately, Ben had been correct, and with his advice, I was able to facilitate two key tackles on deep passes intended for Hunt before half-time.

By the time we entered the visitor's locker room, we were only trailing by three points.

"I think that I saw your girl in the stands next to your parents," Ben teased after the coaches finished giving us their half-time adjustments.

"Hey, can't call her my girl just yet," I said.

"Hang in there. Girls don't make it easy on any of us guys, Blackstone," he said with a chuckle.

"Yeah, whatever. You don't seem to be having any problem," I challenged.

He waggled his finger at me accusingly.

"Don't you be fooled, bro," he said. "I make it look easier, because I started earlier, way before most guys."

I just shook my head as he laughed.

We took the field again, after what seemed like only a handful of minutes.

Our offense managed to maintain control of the football for most of the third quarter, eventually driving in for a touchdown on an eighteen yard run from our running back. He had neatly slipped between the tackles following excellent offensive blocking. Our kicker's extra point gave us a four-point lead, allowing us to breathe a little easier.

By the end of the third quarter, we'd maintained our lead, and I was feeling much more confident about our gameplay. However, I made the mistake of looking up into the stands at Gwen just as the Bison center hiked the ball.

As he had done for most of the game, Hunt flew right past our cornerback in a blur of blue and white and the football sailed perfectly into his hands. By the time that I noticed his reception and ran toward him, he'd run all the way down to our fifteen yard line. My fingers only barely managed to grip his ankle as I tripped while chasing him.

Ben rushed up into my face and pointed to his eyes.

"Dammit, Blackstone! Use those eyeballs for the field and quit stargazing at your girl!"

I felt somewhat embarrassed and ashamed at the same time and the event forced me to do a gut-check regarding my dedication and focus. The whole event made me angry, and I slapped my right palm against my helmet in frustration as I fell back into formation.

Unfortunately, two plays later, the Bison running back dove across the goal line for the touchdown. After the extra point was kicked, we were once again back down by three points.

The coach glared at me with a hard, tight-lipped look as I walked back onto the sidelines. Though silent in his admonishment, I felt like he had just chewed me out. I kept my helmet on and didn't dare gaze back at the stands behind me.

Thanks to our motivated offense, they worked furiously to drive the ball down to the Bison five-yard line. After three more downs, we had to settle for a field goal, but it tied the ball game up for us.

Both teams were even and it was up to one side or the other to take control of the game.

Following the ensuing kickoff, the Bisons ran the ball out to their thirty-three yard line. I jogged out onto the field with a dual sense of dread and steely determination.

Hunt seemed all too aware of his own superiority in the game because I could see him repeatedly scowl at our sophomore cornerback, Benedict, from across the line of scrimmage.

On first down, the Bison running back tried to run, but one of our defensive linemen burst forward and immediately tackled him. On second down, the ball sailed to a third receiver that Ben had to cover, though Ben was able to break up the play by knocking the ball down.

Call it a hunch, but I had a strange feeling that on third down, the ball was destined for Hunt.

I was right.

Hunt hitched to his right, and Benedict tripped, falling to the turf and leaving my area of the field wide open for Hunt. I immediately cut left and bolted toward him, just as Ben had suggested. As I managed to intersect Hunt's position on the field, the football sailed directly between us, and much to my surprise, I managed to catch it by my fingertips as Hunt fell to the ground!

It was like a static charge shot through my body, and I immediately turned to run down the length of the sideline. In an instant, I had become an offensive player.

Ben appeared out of nowhere to take out a tight end that barreled toward me. Our senior cornerback, Yetter, plowed into an offensive tackle who tried to angle in at me. I broke into a dead run like there was a wildfire at my back.

On two more occasions, a teammate appeared to either help block for me or run interference against someone chasing me. In a manner of seconds that felt like minutes, I had raced down the sideline, completely focused on the end zone.

The crowds screamed from both sides of the field, and a blending of players from both teams created a din of shouting ranging from cursing to encouragement. Mostly, I just heard the labored sound of my breathing in my ears as I ran with all my strength toward the looming end zone.

I felt a hand grasp at my left thigh and I nearly lost my balance. But somehow, I managed to cut to my right and half-stagger the remaining distance across the goal line and into the Bison end zone.

Our side of the stands erupted in victorious shouts, while our band pumped out our fight song. I vaguely remembered tossing the ball to a nearby referee before a number of my teammates, including Ben, slapped at my shoulder pads and helmet while shouting at me.

I felt complete redemption for my earlier failures.

My gaze managed to focus on the stands where my parents were shouting and waving their arms over their heads. And then my eyes set upon Gwen, who was standing beside them, her face stricken with a blend of wide-eyed surprise and absolute shock.

"That's how to get it done, Blackstone!" Coach Lambert yelled as I was herded onto our sideline.

For the moment, my earlier faux pas seemed to have been forgiven entirely.

However, my euphoria was short-lived. The Bison team was on offense again, and I had to go out to face an angry-looking Hunt at wide receiver. Only this time, I wasn't feeling hesitant anymore.

Instead, I wanted the ball again.

The Bison offensive series lasted only three downs. On the first two downs, both Ben and I managed to knock the ball down when it was thrown deep into our area. On third down, the Bison offense changed up their receiver formation.

To my surprise, Hunt ran deep into our backfield toward me. The football magically seemed to appear between us, and while I didn't intercept it, I nearly caught it one-handed before it harmlessly bounced to the ground.

Hunt was furious, and he cursed profusely on his way back to his sidelines.

Our offense took control of the football, and our running back fought hard for a few yards each carry, steadily burning the clock. When our kicker lined up for the eventual field goal from the Bison twenty-yard line, the holder pulled a fake and tossed the ball to one of our receivers for a surprising touchdown.

The Bison team fought hard, and eventually managed three points after struggling to get within field goal range. However, our entire defense seemed focused, and by the time that the game ended a few minutes later, we'd won the game by eight points.

After politely lining up for the traditional post-game handshake with Bison, our team dispersed, and I ran over to the sidelines where my parents were standing with Gwen and her mother. They congratulated me, and even Gwen appeared happy for me, though in a decidedly reserved manner.

"Good going. That was…surprising," Gwen awkwardly declared.

Dr. Webber gave her daughter an odd look, and offered, "Nicely done, Scott. We're all very proud of you."

I quickly headed into the locker room. After the coach gave us a quick victory speech and congratulated us, we were all herded back onto the bus for the short ride back to Custer.

Each of us was pumped over the victory, and for the first time, I truly felt like I was finally a *real* member of the team.

* * *

Back at the high school, I showered and changed into a pair of jeans and clean jersey before heading out to the parking lot where I'd left my Blazer. As expected, my parents' SUV was parked next to mine and they were waiting with expectant expressions. I immediately noticed that neither Gwen nor her mother were with them.

"Dinner, anyone?" Mom playfully asked with an arched brow.

"You bet! Let's celebrate with steak tonight," Dad suggested.

Mom frowned at him.

"Hardly fair, Bob," Mom admonished. "Scott's the hero tonight, so he gets to pick."

"It looks like your choice, son," Dad said with a shrug.

"What, are you kidding? Steak sounds great," I heartily agreed.

"Kingston's it is, then," Dad resolved. "Everybody pile in."

Kingston's was renowned as having the town's best steaks and ribs, and it was one of the nicer sit-down restaurants in town, as well.

"Nah, I'll drive over and meet you there," I said.

Having just washed my SUV, I didn't want to leave it sitting around to have its windows soaped by marauding classmates.

"Better hurry up! Last one there gets cold bread," Dad challenged, though he patiently held the passenger door of the SUV open for Mom before hustling around to the driver's side.

I shook my head at him. Dad could be such a goof sometimes.

The window on the passenger side of their SUV rolled down, and Mom leaned out of the window to wink at me.

"No need to rush if you don't want to, Scott," she said.

Just what did she mean by that?

Their SUV pulled forward to reveal Gwen leaning against her gray Sidekick a mere twenty feet away. She gave a cute little wave and offered me a shy smirk.

"Great game, Scott," she said.

"Thanks," I replied, walking over to stand directly before her. "I was surprised to see you there, actually."

"Were you happy to see me?" she asked.

Her question caught me off guard.

"You could say that," I hedged.

"I suppose that I owe you a date," she ventured with a raised brow.

Despite having both met and exceeded her ultimatum, the fact that she had even insisted upon it in the first place, still annoyed me. I felt somewhat resentful, and the original allure of a date with Gwen had become slightly tarnished in my mind.

"Actually, you don't owe me anything," I said.

She frowned and I watched the momentary confusion spread across her face.

"Oh," she said.

"Listen, I need to go meet my parents at Kingston's for dinner," I said, turning away. "Thanks for coming to the game tonight."

"Wait."

I felt her small hand on my shoulder and I turned back to face her.

"Scott, I'm really sorry," she apologized. "I just wanted to see if you were really serious or not about dating me."

I stared into her eyes.

"I was serious," I said, stepping closer to her. "But you need to know that I don't force myself on anyone. I don't go where I'm not wanted."

"You're not forcing me," she countered, leaning forward until her face was mere inches from mine.

The scent from the perfume that she wore was alluring, and I breathed it in. It reminded me of things both soft and sweet.

"I *want* to go out with you, Scott," she said. "I didn't mean to make you think otherwise."

"Then why did you---" I asked.

"I was scared," she blurted, leaning back from me. "I didn't know how to react to you. I don't generally get approached by the other guys in town."

"I'm not other guys," I insisted.

She nodded. "I know that now," she said softly.

Tires screeched into the parking lot, and I turned to see an older model convertible filled with my classmates speed past us.

"Wildcats rule!" squealed a girl whose name I couldn't recall as she tried to stand up in the back seat, only to tumble onto the laps of her laughing friends.

"Kinda' early for that!" I yelled back with a scowl.

When I turned back to Gwen, I was disappointed to see that she had already slipped into the driver's seat of her SUV.

"Hey, wait," I said.

She started the engine and rolled her window down.

"See you tomorrow night, then?" she asked.

"Yeah, sure," I said.

"Make it six o'clock," she said with a smile. "I'll message you my address."

I nodded and a grin formed on my face as her SUV hastily pulled away from me.

Gwen was definitely different from any of the other girls that I had dated before; so much so that I couldn't figure her out. We'd barely met and it was like I was already riding an emotional rollercoaster!

CHAPTER 8

The daylight hours went by in a blur on Saturday. I had some homework to do and then I helped my dad move boxes of merchandise at the grocery store for a couple of hours. By the time I showered and changed into a decent pair of jeans and clean shirt, it was nearly time to leave to pick up Gwen. And for the first time since arriving in Custer, I opened my bottle of cologne.

Mom was talking on the phone when I went downstairs, and she gave me an approving look and the thumbs-up sign.

"Drive carefully," she said. "And have fun!"

I waved as I hurried out the front door.

I had looked up Gwen's address soon after she sent it to me late Friday night. She and her mom lived on a twenty-acre piece of land just east of Custer and south of Stockade Lake Drive. Google Earth indicated that the property was heavily wooded and had a small pond nestled in the trees, not far from the house.

I turned south onto the county road that led from Stockade Lake Drive and alternated between checking my map printout and watching the road. In fact, I almost missed her tree-lined gravel driveway and slammed on my brakes just in time.

Gwen's Sidekick was parked in front of the three-car garage, so I parked my Blazer on the oval-shaped gravel driveway in front of the house.

The house looked relatively new, and it appeared to be a little larger than ours. The flowerbeds were in great shape, which my mom would have approved of; though I had the feeling that my dad would have envied their oversized garage instead.

I walked up to the front door and rang the doorbell, only to hear the subdued sounds of barking from inside the house.

This is it.

I was finally picking up the elusive Gwen Webber for our first date, which made me feel inwardly vindicated given that most of my friends at school had tried to discourage me from trying.

The front door opened and I felt my mouth gape slightly as Gwen stood before me.

"Hi," she greeted with a smile.

She wore a black dress that looked amazing on her. Her dark hair was combed to full length and fell around her face in an attractive manner.

"You look great," I said.

"So do you," she replied.

I heard another bark followed by the hurried skitter of paws on tile, and I looked down to see a brown-colored bulldog sniffing at my jeans.

"Get back, Dundee," Gwen scolded in a firm voice.

I squatted down and gently extended my hand toward the dog. Fortunately, it seemed to like me, and licked my hand after an extended bout of sniffing at it.

"He likes you," she said, squatting down to pat the chunky canine.

I smelled her perfume as she crouched next to me and I tried to be discreet about inhaling the sweet scent.

"How old is he?" I asked.

"Five," she replied. "But he acts just like a puppy."

"Why did you name him Dundee?" I asked, petting the dog, who had already rolled onto his back so that I could scratch his belly.

Though kind of rough-looking initially, he seemed like a nice friendly dog.

"He likes to wander around the property on his own adventures most of the time," she explained. "He's been that way ever since he was a pup, so I named him after the Australian movie character, Crocodile Dundee. Mom still watches those old films from when I was growing up, for some reason."

I was happy to learn something more about Gwen and her family without having to pry it out of her.

Maybe she was finally warming up to me after all.

"Speaking of crocodiles," I began with a raised brow.

She shot me a cross look.

"I *know* what you're going to ask," she interrupted. "Maybe later."

I shrugged.

Dundee ran past me, practically leaping from the porch, and Gwen and I walked out into the front yard as he started sniffing around for somewhere to do his business.

"Nice place," I said for the lack of something cooler to say.

Gwen nodded.

"It's home," she said. "Best of all, it's nice and quiet."

"Your own little escape from the rest of the world?" I asked.

She gave me a sly look and then whistled to get Dundee's attention as he headed for the nearby line of dense shrubs and trees. The dog galloped back over to her and she ushered him back onto the front porch.

"Are you ready to go?" she asked as she opened the front door to let Dundee back inside.

She retrieved a small purse from inside the house, and I held open the door to my SUV for her.

"So, what's the plan for tonight?" she asked as I pulled out onto the country road at the end of her driveway as The Wanted's "Glad You Came" played over the radio.

"How about if I let it be a surprise?" I asked.

She groaned as she pulled the smartphone from her purse.

"I'd love to," she said. "Only I have to text my mom with our destination so that she doesn't call the police out to find me."

I hadn't considered that, though I had to admit that my parents had asked to know earlier that afternoon, as well.

"I was thinking Rapid City for a movie and dinner," I said.

"Don't you mean 'dinner and a movie?'" she asked with arched eyebrows.

I glanced over at her with a curious expression, and then it hit me.

"Hungry?" I asked.

"Way-hungry," she said.

"Okay, dinner, *then* a movie," I confirmed with a nod.

"And the movie?" she asked.

"There's this great action film playing at the Rushmore Mall theater---" I began, but noticed her tight-lipped, dubious expression when I looked at her.

"Or maybe a romantic comedy," I quickly corrected, to which the corners of her mouth upturned slightly.

It occurred to me that being creative with dating plans definitely pivoted on how well one *actually knew* their date.

Then I heard the telltale clicking sounds of her fingernails against her smartphone's screen.

"We're cool," she said finally. "At least until midnight."

I smiled with satisfaction.

It wasn't long after we hit I-385 north toward Rapid City that Gwen and I finally eased into some open and relaxed conversation together.

She told me funny stories about Dundee's exploits over the years, as well as some of the tricks that he'd learned, including briefly balancing on his hind legs when she played certain songs and danced with him.

"You like to dance?" I asked.

"Sure," she said. "You?"

"Uh, maybe when nobody else is looking," I replied.

"Ah, a closet dancer," she said in a mock-conspiratorial manner. "I figured you for one of those."

"Hey, I thought that you once told me that you 'figured me' for football and comics," I said.

"Oh, yeah," she said. "And porn, as I recall."

"Whatever," I chided.

"It's finally all making sense now," she said in serious tone.

I looked up at her.

"What's that?"

"You," she explained. "You're one of those football-comic-closet-porn-dancers!"

We both laughed. And while totally silly, it felt really good to laugh around her, watching her face light up. It was like someone exceptional was awakening from a dormant state.

There was the Gwen that I was enjoying getting to know.

The drive to Rapid City took less than an hour. Being Saturday night, the mall was busy, but I hardly noticed the crowds as I walked alongside Gwen, paying rapt attention to the things that she looked at to try and learn more about what interested her.

I quickly determined that she had an affinity for shoe stores.

Surprise; a girl who likes shoes. Who would have thought it?

As we passed the food court, she said, "Something smells tasty."

I had almost forgotten her comment in the Blazer about her appetite.

Leading the way to the nearest kiosk to peruse the mall's sit-down restaurant options, I suggested a grill called Freddy's that was not far from the food court.

As soon as we sat down beside each other in the cozy corner booth and Digital Daggers' "Head Over Heels" began to play over the restaurant's sound system, I determined that our evening couldn't have started out better.

As Gwen lounged against the cushion of our booth perusing the menu, I ordered chips and salsa and Cokes for us. Her blue eyes looked almost playful when she occasionally glanced over at me.

Nibbling the warm, salty chips that had appeared before us, I thoughtfully considered whether or not she would select a light salad or something bolder.

Food selections on dates were funny things with girls, I had noted. My previous girlfriend, Kelli, would have eaten like a bird and then complained about how full she was afterward.

Then it occurred to me that I had hardly even thought about Kelli since settling in Custer just weeks ago.

Was it because we may not have been such a good fit after all, or was it something else?

Someone else?

"You look deep in thought," Gwen observed.

I shrugged and said, "Just enjoying the time."

She frowned slightly.

"Funny. I thought you were contemplating a guy's eternal conflict of steak versus hamburgers."

I shook my head.

"So lame," I said. "Every guy knows that it's steak whenever you can and hamburgers when you're in a hurry."

"And tonight?" she asked.

"Bacon cheeseburger," I replied. "Cheeseburger, because our movie starts in less than an hour, and bacon, because there's always time to add some pork."

She rolled her eyes at me.

"Now, let me guess," I said. "You're probably busy counting carbs versus calories, right?"

Gwen wrinkled her nose at me.

"I'm getting a chicken sandwich and fries," she said using a 'so there' tone. "And just so you know, I'm ordering it *with* the bun."

"Oooh, you're definitely brave," I teased.

"Bravery runs in my family," she said off-handedly. "Especially in Mom."

"Your mom seems like a really nice person," I said. "I liked her as soon as I met her."

"She said the same thing about you, actually," Gwen observed.

Score one for Dr. Webber.

"Tell me more about your family," I encouraged.

She paused, as if carefully considering what to say, and I worried that she was going to shut down and become reserved on me again.

"After my dad and little brother died in the car accident, I begged Mom to move us to somewhere else," Gwen said in a subdued voice. "Mom kept saying that we had to work through the pain before we made any decisions about moving. Here it is, more than five years later, and we're still in Custer."

I could easily see the emotion reflected in her eyes, and I tried to imagine the level of loss that she must still feel.

"Still working through the pain?" I asked.

She nodded.

"Is that why you keep to yourself so much?"

She looked into my eyes with determination.

"Yes," she said. "That's why it was so hard to finally decide to get to know you better, and why it's still a little hard for me to believe that I'm sitting here with you tonight."

I reached out to cradle her small hand in mine.

"I'm really glad that you did," I said.

She smiled at me, allowing me to gently hold her hand.

"Me, too," she whispered.

Our meal arrived and we dove into our food so that we could finish in time for the start of the movie.

By the time we made it to the theater inside the mall, the stores had all closed. However, we were able to see both the previews and the film; a romantic comedy titled *Town Asunder* about a corporate raider who returned to his hometown to repossess all of the city-owned buildings, only to fall in love with a girl he'd known in high school, who just happened to be the town's mayor.

It was a bizarre, but funny, film. Best of all, Gwen's mood lightened up again and she really seemed to enjoy it.

Everything was going great. At least, until I saw a group of kids from school, including Tammy, one of the girls who had recently written harassing comments on Gwen's windshield. They stared at us, whispering back and forth between each other as we passed.

Tammy, in particular, spared a sidelong glare for me.

Gwen ignored them, but I gave Tammy a long, hard look that pointedly warned 'stay away.'

Not that I expected any trouble from them while at the mall. My concern was that I wanted them to continue keeping their distance from Gwen once we returned to town.

I didn't like seeing people being harassed, especially those that I cared about.

The parking lot was relatively devoid of cars when we exited the mall, which made it easy to find my Blazer.

The night sky was clear, and I briefly looked up at the partial moon phase that loomed overhead.

"Are you a stargazer?" she asked as I held the passenger door open for her.

"Not much, until recently," I replied. "Back in Springfield, you couldn't see as many of the stars as you can in Custer."

"It's the light pollution," she commented before I shut the door.

I thought about that as I walked around to the driver's side. It was another nice aspect of moving to Custer that I hadn't considered until Gwen had mentioned it.

Maybe living in Custer while finishing high school wasn't going to turn out so badly after all.

"You're the first girl that I've known who talks about stars," I noted as we pulled out of the parking lot to head toward the highway.

"Is that a bad thing?" she asked, staring at me.

"Not at all," I confidently replied.

We talked about music and movies most of the drive back to Custer. But following a brief lull in the conversation, I ventured into a topic that I'd been skirting for quite some time with her.

"Hey, talk to me about alligators," I suggested.

As I looked over at her, she stared back at me with a suspicious expression.

"They're reptiles with lots of teeth," she said off-handedly. "There's even a fashion company named Lacoste that uses them for their company logo. You should try Googling it sometime."

"C'mon, Miss Sarcasm," I said. "You know what I'm talking about."

"I'll think about it and get back to you," she said.

I let the topic lie, not wanting to press the issue and upset her, so I changed the subject to music again. The topics of Lady Gaga and reality television were far more approachable for discussion, it seemed. Although I was hardly well-versed in the latest competition among contestants for some singing competition reality show that she talked about.

When I pulled up in front of her house, it was just after eleven-thirty. Fortunately, we'd managed to respect her mom's midnight curfew.

I got out and walked around to the passenger side to open her door for her.

"I had a really great time," Gwen offered as she exited the vehicle.

"I'm glad," I replied. "Me, too."

We stood there for a moment, and I stared into her eyes, relishing how beautiful they looked. She broke my gaze by looking up at the sky, which caused me to do the same.

It was a breathtaking array of lights above us; so many more that I had ever seen living in Springfield, or anywhere else, for that matter.

When I looked back at her, she was already staring up at me in an endearing manner.

"I'm sorry about the gator question," I said. "I won't ask again---"

She reached up and placed her index finger against my lips. "Shh. It's okay," she said softly, withdrawing her finger. "Soon."

I'm good with that.

"Go out with me again," I said.

"Definitely," she whispered.

Her front door opened, revealing a bemused-looking Dr. Webber clad in jeans and a sweatshirt.

"I thought that I heard somebody pull up out front," she said.

Wonderful timing.

"I'll message you," Gwen assured me as she stepped around the front of my SUV to head to her front porch.

"Sounds good," I said, walking back around to the driver's side. "Goodnight."

Gwen gave me one of her cute half-waves before following her mom back into the house.

As I pulled out of her driveway, I was already looking forward to seeing her again.

* * *

I slept late on Sunday, but had to mow and edge the lawn before my day was free. During the afternoon, I drove over to Rushmore Burgers on the west side of town to meet Ben and a couple of my teammates for lunch. We commandeered a table outside and were waiting for our orders to arrive when I heard my name called.

"Hey, Scott!" Came a girl's voice.

I turned to see a table of four girls, all Custer cheerleaders, sitting not far from us. One of the girls, Crissy, urgently waved at me.

"C'mere a minute," she beckoned.

Crissy and I had two classes together, and she was one of the first people to introduce herself when I arrived at the high school. We got along great, though the vibe that had formed between us felt more like friendship than anything else.

"He catches one interception for a touchdown, and now he's got our cheerleaders all calling for him," chided Sutton, one of our junior linebackers.

"Well, then, just make an interception," I said with a shrug as I rose from the table.

"Oh, burn," scoffed VanHorn, who sat next to Sutton.

Ben laughed.

I squatted down beside where Crissy was sitting and she smiled at me.

"So, what's this I hear about you dating Gwen Webber?" she asked.

Her friends watched me intently as I grinned and absently rubbed at my partly-stubble chin.

"Why's that so interesting?" I asked.

She shrugged.

"Just askin'," she replied. "But by the look on your face, it must have gone really well."

"I don't kiss and tell, but yeah, we went out last night," I said. "And we had a good time."

"Well, I've got to give you points for that little feat," she said.

"Still, there's about as much future there as trying to date a Rusher or Passer," said the blonde-haired girl sitting next to Crissy.

"Good one, Misty," said another girl.

I stared at Misty and looked at Crissy with a perplexed look.

"Nobody's told you about Rushers and Passers, have they?" Crissy asked. "We're not talkin' football here, newbie."

I just shook my head.

"Rushers are what we call the tourists who stop in town on their way to see Mount Rushmore," she explained. "Most of the Rushers are foreigners."

"And Passers are people who are passing through for other reasons," Misty spoke up. "You know, camping, fishing, or stuff like that."

Honestly, it seemed a little weird to me, but whatever.

"Okay," Crissy said. "But back to Gwen."

I shrugged.

"She's pretty cool, actually," I said. "I like her; a lot."

"Okie-dokie," she said. "Don't say that I didn't try to warn you."

"People around here really don't like her very much," I observed acidly.

"Hey, I'm not tryin' to pick a fight here," Crissy said. "We're friends, Scott. You're a really nice guy, and I just don't want to see you get hurt, that's all."

I just stared at her with a dubious expression.

"Listen, Gwen's never done anything bad to me, and I don't have a grudge against her or anything," Crissy said. "But people talk, and there's been a rumor for years that she had something to do with her brother's death."

"But, Dr. Webber said that they died in a car accident," I countered.

"Yeah," Misty spoke up. "Well, did she tell you that Gwen was also in that accident five years ago? It's said that both she and her brother, Tommy, were alive after the accident. Granted, Tommy had been injured, but something happened before the emergency vehicles arrived. Supposedly, passersby who stopped to help saw something that scared their wits out of them."

"Something about Gwen?" I pressed.

Misty shrugged. "So it seems. But exactly *what* that was seems to be under debate. Whatever it was, it changed Gwen, and she closed herself off from everyone in town after that. It was like she just shut down. I remember back when she used to go to school and she was pretty friendly. Ever since the accident, she hardly says a word to anyone."

"That's pretty awful," I said.

Neither Dr. Webber nor Gwen had mentioned those details to me.

"Anyway, I just thought that you should know more about what you might be getting into, that's all," Crissy offered.

"Thanks," I replied politely.

I didn't actually doubt Crissy's good intentions, but I knew better than to accept everything at face value. I'd already learned that many in town were overly critical about Gwen. There seemed to be a lot of misunderstandings about her, actually.

"Well, whoever you date, just don't end up being a Custerstodian," said the brunette sitting to the right of Misty.

"A what?" I asked.

"Those are people who spend their entire lives stuck here in Custer," Crissy explained.

"Birth to death," Misty chimed in with a grin.

I nodded. It wasn't like I intended to end up as a Custerstodian.

"Hey, interception hero," Sutton called from our table. "I'm fixin' to take your fries if you don't get back over here."

"Thanks for the info," I said.

My teammates all stared at me as I took a seat.

"What was that all about?" Ben asked.

Unwrapping my steak sandwich, I shrugged.

"Just learning a little bit more about this town," I said.

In truth, I had a lot more left to learn about Custer and its residents. And, of course, Gwen.

CHAPTER 9

By Monday, the week quickly turned busy again. The following days were filled with classes, both online and in person, as well as what seemed like tons of homework. It was crazy how much homework the teachers were always dishing out to us.

It seemed like I had a million things to take care of between school and home obligations. Never mind that I had football practice during the afternoons and into the early evenings.

Honestly, I couldn't figure out how my parents could get away with telling me, "Enjoy things now, Scott. Just wait; it gets even busier when you become an adult."

They had to be kidding, right?

Even worse, was that I kept thinking about Gwen and what Crissy and Misty had told me on Sunday. I wanted to just call or go over to visit Gwen and ask her about everything. However, I realized how sensitive the topic was, and I wasn't about to charge headfirst into things.

The topic needed to be handled delicately.

But, how?

Until I had a good answer to that question, the very least that I could do was ask Mom. She *did* work for Dr. Webber, after all.

Since Mom had to work late at the hospital on Monday, Tuesday evening was my first opportunity to talk to her.

"Good meatloaf, Mom," I offered.

"You mean, you actually tasted it before you swallowed it whole?" Dad teased.

"You taught me everything I know, Dad," I said with a grin.

Mom laughed.

"He's got you there, Bob," she said.

"I'm in a houseful of comedians," he mumbled.

"So, Mom, I've got a quick question," I said, neatly changing the subject. "Have you heard any details about the accident that Dr. Webber's husband and son were killed in?"

Mom looked up with a peculiar expression.

"Just what Olivia told us," she said. "It's not a topic that has come up, actually. Why do you ask?"

I shrugged.

"No reason," I replied. "Somebody at school mentioned it recently."

Then I quickly shoveled some meatloaf into my mouth.

"You know," Dad began. "Emma Walston, Betty's daughter who operates her mother's bakery in town, said something to me at the grocery store over a week ago. For some reason, it seems that some people have been talking about the accident recently."

"What did she say?" I asked expectantly.

Mom glanced at me and then stared at my dad.

"Emma didn't say a lot, really," he said. "Just that it was such a shame what happened, and how terrible the changes in Gwen were after the accident."

I nodded.

Well, it's something, but not the kind of details that I want to hear more about.

"Have you considered asking Gwen about it?" Mom asked.

"Yeah, but I didn't want to upset her," I said.

Mom arched her eyebrow in that manner that she did

when I wasn't thinking things through as much as she would have liked.

"I'd imagine that Gwen would be more upset if you asked everyone else but her," she ventured.

I nodded.

She made a good point. Mom had a knack for getting to the base level of things.

That evening, I typed a message to Gwen asking if she was free to get together on Saturday.

Late Thursday night, Gwen responded that she looked forward to us getting together then. She also said that she and her mom planned to be at our home game against the Belle Fourche Broncs on Friday.

For the most part, things were looking up.

All that I had to do was help our team win against a tough opponent on Friday and figure out some way to gently broach the subject of the accident with Gwen.

Despite the logic in Mom's earlier comment, a sense of dread filled me at the thought of talking to Gwen about that topic. Dealing with emotional or finesse issues were never my strength. I was definitely more of a doer.

At the very least, helping us win against the Broncs didn't sound so tough anymore by comparison.

* * *

The stadium seats were once again full on Friday evening for our game against Belle Fourche. Their side of the field was arrayed with their purple and white team colors, and a large number of their fans and supporters showed up for the game, holding the promise for a loud environment.

That's okay. I like the crowd noise; it pumps me up even more.

The Broncs offense won the coin toss and got the football at kickoff, but we managed to force a three-and-out on their first drive. After that, our offense controlled the clock for about half of the first quarter, methodically working down the field until our running back, Sturm, slipped between the tackles on the Broncs two-yard line for a touchdown.

By the end of the first quarter, I spotted Gwen sitting in the stands sitting between her mother and my dad. She appeared to be enjoying herself, and I saw her laugh after Dad said something to her.

It was really great to see her having a good time.

At half-time, we were ahead by ten points, and I was feeling confident about my abilities to guard my portion of the field. I'd broken up a number of deep passes that'd been thrown my way and Ben and I each had a number of key tackles to show for our efforts. Coach Lambert was happy with the way most of us were playing, though he spoke somewhat critically about one of our receivers, Chavez, who was having trouble sticking to his routes.

As we ran out onto the field for the second half, Gwen yelled my name, and I looked up at her as she waved her arms at me. Given her tendency to be subdued, it was great to see her acting somewhat animated in public.

I was stoked about her enthusiasm, actually.

The third quarter was a blur as our teams traded the ball back and forth. The Broncs seemed a little desperate by the end of the quarter, and some of the players started playing a little dirty. One of their special formation receivers deliberately tripped me up in tight coverage, though the refs missed the call against him. That brought a series of boos from the crowd, as well as some shouting at the refs from Coach Lambert.

Fortunately, one of our cornerbacks, Benedict, picked the Broncs receiver up for the tackle soon after the reception.

Despite the Broncs' efforts, we kept a touchdown lead by the start of the fourth quarter. That's when my adrenaline amped up more. Even the crowd's energy levels intensified. It was as if I could feel the desperation rolling like waves from the Broncs' players as they strove to take the ball from our offense.

That's when the turnover occurred.

It was a clean hand-off to Sturm on third down from Fuller, our quarterback. Sturm handled the ball like a pro, but he failed to see the Broncs safety as he hit him from his blind spot, knocking the football out of his grasp. Unfortunately, there was also a Broncs tackle in the area that fell upon the ball like a collapsed wall.

With only nine minutes left in the game, the Broncs offense started their march in our end of the field. They were in easy striking range to tie up the game.

It was apparent that they were hungry for a touchdown, but I was determined to do everything that I could do to get the ball back for us, or at the very least, hold them to a field goal.

We held them on three downs to only eight yards, and our entire defense was nicely bunched up to help support each other. I hoped that the Broncs would settle for the field goal and then try to get the ball back. However, it was an excellent time for a trick play, and I was feeling really edgy about the prospect.

On fourth down, the Broncs didn't even call a time out; they just kept their offense on the field and set their formation.

"Just don't let them get behind you!" Ben yelled to me and our two corners.

Fourth and two.

It was the moment when great plays were made and great players stepped up for their team and fans alike.

The Broncs receiver who I was covering, a guy named Royce, burst off of the line like a jet and quickly distanced himself from the cornerback that was covering him. In fact, despite my best effort to pick him up, he nearly ran right past me toward our end zone. I just knew that the ball was intended for him, but rather than look over my shoulder to check, I focused on running hard to catch up with him.

I managed to catch up to Royce in the middle of our end zone, just as the football darted into the corner of my vision. I leapt up to battle for the football, but Royce grasped it first and spun around to secure it.

I managed to twist one of my arms around his body in a futile attempt to knock the ball loose. We both fell back down to the turf; only he landed directly on top of me. My breath was knocked from my lungs as I hit the ground and Royce's body slammed into me from above.

The Custer crowd went wild amidst shouts, whistles, and hoots.

My ears rang as the sounds around me grew muted and my scope of vision shrank into a dwindling circle. My lungs ached as I strained to take in a breath. A few seconds later, the sounds of the crowd returned as the ringing in my ears subsided. Ben and Benedict stood above me looking down as the Coach and a paramedic squatted down next to me while two of the referees looked on.

"You okay, son?" the coach asked.

I slowly nodded, trying to get my bearings.

After the quick assessment of my condition, they helped me sit up. Then, with their assistance, I rose to my feet and both the home and visiting crowds supportively clapped.

At the paramedic's recommendation, I methodically walked to our side of the field. Only then did I realize that Royce hadn't been able to hold onto the ball. Our offense was already out on the field in our 'burn the clock' formation.

"Way to go, Blackstone!" Ben congratulated me as I made my way to the bench.

To my surprise, Dr. Webber was already there waiting with Mom beside her.

"Take a seat, Scott, and I'll have a look at you," Dr. Webber said.

"But, I'm fine," I retorted, only to see Mom give me a hard look.

It was one of those awkward moments when having a mother who was also a registered nurse double-trumped any retort that I could've come up with.

I plopped down onto the bench and allowed Dr. Webber to examine my reflexes.

"You gave us all a little scare," she said.

"I'm proud of you, son!" shouted my dad from somewhere behind me.

Once again, Mom gave a hard look, only this time it was directed at my father.

"What do ya' think, Doc?" I asked as Dr. Webber shined a small penlight into my eyes.

"Well, you seem okay, but let's schedule a follow-up with you next week," she said. "Your mother will arrange everything for you when we get back into the office on Monday."

The coach stopped by briefly to check in with Dr. Webber as I sipped on some Gatorade that had been handed to me. He nodded at me and reached down to retrieve my helmet.

"Aww, c'mon, Coach," I pleaded.

"Doctor's orders," he replied with a shrug, handing my helmet off to one of our assistant coaches. "Don't worry; I think that our offense has this game in the bag for us."

I glanced over my shoulder to see my dad and Gwen waving back at me; both of them wearing a huge grin. I waved back and made my way to where my teammates were bunched up on the sidelines to watch our offense. As Coach Lambert had said, Sturm held onto the football with a vice-like grip and pounded into the Broncs defense with a vengeance. I could tell that the turnover had angered him, and he was taking out his frustration on the Broncs.

Fortunately, he kept his compose, and with a great blocking effort by our offensive tackles, slipped through gaps to eat up both yardage and the remaining minutes on the clock.

In fitting fashion, Sturm ran into the Broncs end zone in the last twenty seconds of the game. The air went completely out of the Broncs and their quarterback graciously took a knee following the kick-off so that the remaining few seconds ticked away.

We won by two touchdowns!

The stadium howled as our band played out our school song. The coaches met at mid-field for parting words as both teams lined up to shake hands.

"Get ya' next time," Royce promised with a respectful nod as we quickly clasped hands.

Gwen ran up to give me a hug as I walked off the field.

"You did a great job, Scott," she congratulated me. "Are you okay?"

My pulse raced as she hugged me and I breathed in the sweet scent of her perfume. Despite the growing achiness in my body, I was so happy, that even if my body had been racked with pain, I wouldn't have complained a bit.

"Thanks, I'm good," I said. "And I'm really glad that you came to the game."

She gently disengaged from our hug.

"Well, the game is growing on me, I suppose," she said while wrinkling her nose. "Although, I can't say much for the post-game aromas."

I chuckled.

Dad patted me on the back as I turned to head to the locker room.

"You played a great game, son!" he beamed. "I'm proud of you."

That made me feel pretty good, too.

Everybody was in high spirits in the locker room, and the coach told us that we were coming together to be a real presence in the district this year. Many of my teammates congratulated me on the key play against Royce late in the game.

"Thanks," Sturm offered. "You really helped to redeem me out there, Blackstone. I won't forget that."

"Hey, I see a special slot receiver in our future," touted Chavez.

That meant a lot coming from our star receiver.

My new life in Custer was definitely coming together better than I could've expected. Although, I realized that Gwen was easily part of the reason.

After changing into blue jeans and a clean jersey, I joined my parents, Dr. Webber, and Gwen at Pizza Palace. A number of my teammates and their girlfriends had gathered there, as well.

We had a great time, and Gwen seemed to come out of her shell quite a bit. She traded puns with my dad on a few occasions and genuinely seemed to ignore some of the strange looks that were cast her way by a few of Custer's residents who curiously regarded us.

CHAPTER 10

Upon waking early on Saturday morning, my first thoughts were of Gwen. I anxiously anticipated seeing her again.

Per her request, I was to go over to her house later that afternoon. She'd been vague about what our plans were supposed to be, only saying that I should dress really comfortably.

Was that the same as casual?

I didn't care; I would've dressed in a tuxedo. Of course, comfortable was better.

Better yet, I'll ask Mom.

Dad was no expert when the question went beyond what suit to wear.

That morning, I went up to the school to work out on the equipment in the weight room, but still the clock just wouldn't tick fast enough for my preference. Unfortunately, when I got back home, Dad had more than enough ideas for filling my spare time. Between helping him move boxes of merchandise at the grocery store and assisting with inventory at the convenience store, there was hardly a minute available for boredom.

I finished cleaning up and changed into jeans and a vintage Foo Fighters concert T-shirt. Then I went downstairs to find my parents looking over account logs from the grocery store together.

"Well? Comfortable?" I asked.

"That's certainly comfortable-looking," Mom said.

"Sweatpants are even more comfortable," Dad chimed in.

Mom frowned at him and shook her head, so I felt confident that I'd received the proper advice.

I pulled into Gwen's driveway right at four-thirty. I'd barely pressed her doorbell when the front door swept open to reveal Gwen casually holding her watch before her with a raised eyebrow.

I took the opportunity to appreciate how good she looked in faded jeans and black and purple knit top.

"You almost had me worried there," she teased.

"Oh, hush," I said, reaching out to tickle her.

Gwen giggled, retreating inside as her bulldog, Dundee, barked and happily wagged his tail. She sidestepped me and playfully swatted at my hands as I entered.

"You're in a no-tickling zone now," she declared.

"Nice home," I observed, glancing into the living room.

"Thanks," she said. "Mom's part interior decorator and part doctor, it seems. Last year, the hospital administrators asked her pick out some of the new furniture and décor for the offices."

The women in the Webber family were just as full of surprises as they were of mysteries, it seemed.

I couldn't help but notice all of the healthy-looking plants decorating the living room.

"Somebody has a real green thumb thing going on," I quipped.

"That's Mom," Gwen replied.

"I'm not the plant nurturing type, it seems," she added somewhat ruefully.

I noted her somewhat somber-looking expression.

"I'm not much on plants, myself. Mom's the green thumb in our house, too," I offered. "So, what's the plan for this afternoon?"

"Well, first of all, good job dressing comfortably," she observed. "You look like a respectable roadie."

I frowned, dubiously glancing down at my jeans and T-shirt.

"Actually, you look great," she added with smirk. "C'mon, let's talk about *the plan*."

Her added comment bolstered my confidence.

I followed her into the kitchen, where she turned on the oven and reached into the refrigerator for a foil-covered pan. She placed it into the oven with an exaggerated flourish.

"Dinner is now being prepared," she said. "Mom helped me put it together this morning."

"And dinner would be?"

"A surprise," she said. "Meanwhile, you get to have the cola of your choice; meaning either Coke or Sprite."

I grinned and accepted a Coke as she pulled out a Sprite for herself.

Then she reached out to take me by the hand and led me through the house to the back door leading outside. On her way out the door, she grabbed a small portable speaker that had an iPod dangling from it.

"Stay, Dundee," she ordered, carefully closing the door behind us.

"Dundee doesn't get to come?" I asked.

"Not this time," she said.

Her covered patio held a perfect view to the forest behind their house. Along one side of her yard, a relatively wide grassy path sloped down an incline for about fifty yards.

We proceeded down the path to an open grassy area interspersed with medium and tall trees that sheltered the shoreline of a small, slightly murky-looking pond. It looked like there was a small, partially dried up creek at the back of the pond that wound further into the trees.

A large, flat-topped boulder, long and wide enough for me to lay down upon, sat partially-buried at the edge of the pond.

Gwen led me over to the boulder and perched atop it.

"Have a seat," she said.

I sat beside her, taking in the sight of the peaceful, yet strange, area before us.

She switched on her iPod, and Aimee Mann's "Save Me" began to play.

"This is where I come to contemplate," Gwen said. "And read."

I chuckled.

"You seem to read almost anywhere," I said.

"True enough," she agreed. "Except at football games."

"Glad to hear that."

Save for the sound of the breeze rustling the trees, we sat in silence, basking in the relatively warm late summer sunshine.

I had to admit that it was a very relaxing spot, and I momentarily wondered if the pond was stocked with fish.

"If I share something really private with you, can you keep my secret, Scott?" Gwen asked in a mysterious tone.

I turned to her and saw the searching look in her eyes.

"Of course, I can," I assured her.

She regarded me with an arched brow.

"Look around," she said.

My eyes once again swept the peaceful scene surrounding us. Then I noticed a partially submerged object in the pond, not far offshore from where we were sitting.

It was an object with eyes and a snout!

"Damn! That's the—" I nearly shouted as I grasped at her arm, ready to leap from the boulder with her in tow.

It was the animal that I'd first seen with her at the lake. I was shocked at how stealthily it had maneuvered close to us. Gwen put her hand on my arm in calming fashion.

I stared at the creature, which had to be well over six feet in length.

"He's my pet alligator," she calmly stated. "Well, former pet, anyway. Oh, and just for the record, he's an alligator, not a crocodile."

My heart was beating a mile a minute, but I managed to settle back onto the boulder next to Gwen.

"Isn't that kind of dangerous? Those things eat people, you know," I warned.

"It's okay. I'm able to safely influence him," she insisted.

"Oh, really? How do you do that, exactly?" I asked.

It wasn't as if I wanted to call her a liar, but she was hardly a match for the toothy reptile before us. Though in truth, I probably wasn't either.

She shrugged.

"Mom and I both have a way with animals, you could say," she hedged.

"More secrets?" I asked, wholly curious as to what she meant by that.

"Some secrets take time, Scott," she replied. "This isn't easy for me, you know."

I reached up to gently touch the side of her soft face.

"I'm not going anywhere," I replied, though I pensively stared sidelong at the alligator.

She reached up to grasp my hand in both of hers.

"I hope that's true," she said. "After the accident, I really never thought that I could even try to get close to someone else again. Except for Mom, of course."

I frowned.

"Why not?" I asked. "What changed?"

She looked away from me to stare into the distance.

"I don't think it's a good idea for people to get close to me," she replied. "I still don't think that you should either, now that I'm starting to have feelings for you."

Despite her revelation about having feelings for me, I frowned.

"I don't understand, Gwen," I said.

"I'm sorry," she replied after a heavy sigh. "I'm not ready to talk about that just yet."

I politely nodded, though I was dying of curiosity.

"Okay," I said. "But I hope that you know that you can trust me, Gwen."

My attention quickly returned to the alligator. Call it self-preservation, but despite what Gwen said, I didn't trust the animal to maintain a safe distance.

"Well, you can at least tell me about *it*," I said, pointing to the creature. "How did you get it? Where did it come from?"

"When I was a little girl, my father gave *him* to me," she explained. "The plan had been to give him to the Reptile Gardens near Rapid City once he got too big. But after Daddy and my brother, Tommy, died, I just didn't have the heart to donate him. He was like a last remaining link to my father. So, I turned him loose in our pond. After I finally proved to Mom that I could manage him, she was okay with it after awhile, but she rarely comes down here to see him."

I looked at Gwen and then back at the creature, which had floated slightly closer to the shoreline. Frankly, while I tried not to doubt her word on the matter, it was still a fairly unnerving revelation.

Who keeps a full-sized pet alligator?

"What's his name?" I asked.

"His name is Chewie."

Chewie?

I didn't think that I liked the connotations of that name.

"So, um, what do you feed Chewie, exactly?" I asked.

"Oh, I don't have to feed him very often," she said. "Usually, he eats fish, birds, and smaller animals around the pond. Occasionally, when it rains enough to fill the creek, he sneaks into Stockade Lake. The creek snakes its way westward and south until it reaches the lake. There's just a lot more for him to feed on there. He's only done it a few times, but the moment I notice he's gone, I go looking for him. The day that you first saw me at the lake, I was herding him back up the creek."

That shocked me. Just how did Gwen manage to herd an alligator?

"*You* herded *him*?" I demanded.

"What can I say? Mom and I have sort of a special

influence over animals," she said.

I definitely couldn't wait to learn more about that.

"Yeah? Like how?" I asked suspiciously.

"Watch," she said.

Gwen lifted her right arm up and pointed it in the direction of the alligator with her palm held upright and outward toward him. I watched Gwen, only to see a blank expression on her face. She rotated her palm in a small waving fashion while sweeping her arm to the right.

I felt a fleeting wave of weakness sweep through my body along with a quick chill. At the same moment, Chewie splashed in the water and made a low growling noise as he swished off in the direction that Gwen had moved her arm.

That was really weird.

"Whoa," I said. "*What* did you just do?"

"Let's just say it's an acquired skill and leave it at that," she said evasively.

"Yeah, but *how* did you do that?" I pressed. "And can your mom do that, too?"

"Probably, but I'd rather not talk about it," she insisted. "I shouldn't even have shown you that."

"Well, you kind of just *did* show me," I countered.

"Scott, *please*, let's talk about something else," she urged.

I paused to gather my wits over what I'd just seen. Surely it'd been some sort of trick with her hand, but that didn't explain the weird feeling that I felt go through my body.

"Uh, so, Chewie's never attacked anyone?" I asked, anxious to find out as much as I could. "Or maybe gone after Dundee?"

Gwen shook her head.

"Not at all," she affirmed. "Dundee doesn't come down here very often from what I've seen. And there's never been any report of Chewie attacking anyone. He stays relatively hidden here in the pond for the most part, and it's only limited times during the year when he can make it up the creek to the lake and back. In fact, he's never come up close our house, either."

I couldn't help but wonder about small children or pets in town being threatened by Chewie if he wandered away from the pond or creek. In truth, I was surprised to hear that nobody had been attacked thus far. Still, it didn't make me feel more comfortable about that fact.

"Okay, well, I did some research on alligators," I began.

"Somehow, I thought that you might have," she said.

"Anyway, the winters here in South Dakota seem like they would kill old Chewie here," I ventured.

"This pond has some sort of hot springs feeding it," Gwen said. "The water stays abnormally warm year around, and that keeps Chewie warm enough in the winter to survive. He seems to like to stay around here most of the year, anyway."

I pensively glanced once more at the alligator.

Thankfully, he hadn't moved closer to us. I didn't relish the idea of trying to fend off a dangerous alligator; not that I wouldn't try if I needed to in order to defend Gwen, of course.

Come to think of it, weren't virtually all alligators considered to be dangerous?

We watched Chewie in silence as he fully submerged under the pond surface and disappeared.

"You don't think that I'm too weird, do you?" Gwen asked timidly.

I looked at her, and she appeared so vulnerable and sensitive at that moment as she stared back at me with a sad-looking expression.

"Yes, you're very weird for having a pet alligator," I teased. "But I still like you…a lot."

I wrapped my arm around her shoulders, and she leaned in against me.

"I'm glad to hear that," she said, relief evident in her voice.

"One minor mystery solved, at least," I said.

I didn't want to spoil the moment by asking more about the accident that had resulted in her father and brother's death, or pressing her further about the ability that she claimed she and her mother had over animals.

Instead, I asked, "It seems like there's always another mystery to solve, doesn't it?"

"I suppose," she replied with a sigh, nestling closer against me as she held my hand while I encircled her shoulders with my other arm.

Alligator or no, and despite my lingering questions, I decided that sitting beside Gwen was a great way to spend the remainder of the afternoon.

A few minutes later, Chewie reappeared not far from the shoreline, though he seemed content to just lie still in the water like some floating log.

We sat together in silence while the afternoon sun faded into early evening as Death Cab for Cutie's "Underneath the Sycamore" played. The alligator finally submerged, and with a swish of its tail beneath the surface, disappeared from view again.

Around six o'clock, my stomach growled and Gwen pulled away from me.

"Hungry?" she asked.

"You bet," I replied.

With a final look over my shoulder to see if the alligator was stalking us, we returned to the house to find Gwen's mother in the kitchen preparing a tossed salad. I immediately smelled the aroma of something that suggested Italian might be for dinner.

"I thought that you two might be heading this way before long," she remarked.

"Hi, Dr. Webber," I offered.

"How are you feeling today, Scott?"

"I feel great. Back to normal," I replied.

"Good," she said. "We'll verify that next week, of course. How does lasagna sound for dinner?"

"Great," I enthusiastically replied.

"Excellent," she said. "Because that's what we're serving tonight."

"Mom, please," Gwen groaned.

"I'm just saying," she said innocently. "Why don't you two wash up while I finish up here?"

Once the three of us sat down to dinner, Gwen's mom served the salad, lasagna, and slices of garlic bread. Everything smelled great, and I found that my appetite was heartier than I first thought down by the pond.

The pond with the alligator in it.

"So, Gwen introduced me to Chewie today," I said.

"Gwen mentioned to me earlier today that she intended to do that," Dr. Webber observed. "And happily, it appears that you survived the grand unveiling," she added with a smirk.

"He's a good-sized croc," I said, using my best mock-Australian accent.

"Gator," Gwen corrected.

Gwen's mother chuckled.

"Well, don't get too used to seeing Chewie," she cautioned. "I've mentioned to Gwen recently that it might be time for Chewie to find a permanent home at Reptile Gardens, as we intended a number of years ago."

"*Mom!*" Gwen exclaimed.

Her mother adopted a serious expression, and challenged, "Now, Gwen. We've talked about this before. If he decides to go up the creek someday, that only increases the danger of a potentially bad encounter with someone."

I glanced at Gwen, suddenly realizing that Dr. Webber seemed unaware of Chewie's exploits.

Gwen frowned at me and shook her head slightly in warning.

"I've got him under control," Gwen insisted. "He's trained."

"That's silly. He's a wild animal," Dr. Webber mildly chastised. "And you can't ever completely be sure that he won't do something dangerous when you're not around to watch over him."

It sounded as if Gwen's mother wasn't as completely on

board as Gwen had alluded earlier.

"Dad gave him to *me*," Gwen insisted. "It should be my decision."

"Your father always intended for Chewie to find a safer home among his own kind once he got big enough," Dr. Webber said. "You can always visit him at Reptile Gardens; it's only as far as Rapid City. They can give also provide him with a stable diet. The pond's too small to support him now that he's grown."

Gwen looked at me with a helpless expression. However, I remained quiet during the exchange. The subject was better left between the two of them; it wasn't my place to interfere. Though, in truth, I sort of sided with Gwen's mother on the matter. Chewie easily seemed potentially dangerous, in my opinion.

I briefly considered that perhaps my reluctance was because I didn't have a comfort zone built up with him yet.

On second thought, that's stupid. He's dangerous.

Gwen withdrew into her plate, picking at her salad and lasagna. Gwen's mother politely smiled at me, but then cast a pointed, disapproving look at her daughter.

Dundee seemed oblivious to the subdued mood; he frequently pawed at my leg and looked up at me to beg for samples from my plate.

"Dundee, stop begging. You eat more than enough of your own food," Gwen's mother admonished the bulldog after a few minutes.

Eventually, Dundee lay down at Gwen's feet, sulking much the same way that Gwen was.

"So, Scott, what are your thoughts about next Friday's game?" Dr. Webber asked.

I chatted about our upcoming game against Lead-Deadwood, but Gwen remained seemingly oblivious, focused on her plate before her. I felt bad for her, and tried to bring her into the conversation, but she remained relatively quiet throughout the meal.

After we finished eating, Gwen and her mother started

clearing the table, though I helped bring some dishes to the sink. The atmosphere felt awkward and I wasn't really sure what to do with myself.

"Dessert, anyone?" Gwen's mother asked as she picked up a foil-covered pan from the counter. "They're homemade brownies."

I loved brownies.

My mouth watered at the prospect of them, but I noticed Gwen leaning against the kitchen counter with her arms folded before her. It was obvious to me that she was in a protracted bad mood.

"No, thank you," Gwen flatly said, to which her mother cast a reproving look.

"I, uh, should probably get going, Dr. Webber," I said. "Maybe next time. Dinner was really great, though, and I appreciate you having me over."

"Oh, well, you're very welcome, Scott," Dr. Webber replied as she sat the pan back onto the counter. "Thank you for coming over. But would you mind keeping Chewie our little secret for the time being? He's going to be addressed in the near future, and I would rather not give the town another reason to gossip."

"Sure. I understand completely," I replied, noting that Gwen was furiously staring at her mom.

"Well, Gwen?" Dr. Webber expectantly asked.

"Thanks for coming over, Scott. I'll walk you out," Gwen offered half-heartedly.

"No need, I've got it," I said, quickly retreating toward the front door. "Message me later, Gwen, and thanks again. I had fun today."

During my drive home, I reflected on both the strange and wonderful aspects of my afternoon with Gwen. And while I'd finally learned the backstory on the alligator, I was still left with so many more questions.

"Chewie?" I asked aloud, shaking my head over the odd choice for his name.

CHAPTER 11

On Sunday, I spent the morning and part of the mid-afternoon fishing with my dad on the shores of Bismark Lake, which is a smaller lake located just a few miles north of Stockade Lake. It was a beautiful day for fishing, and both of us had caught a few bass, crappie, and even a trout or two by lunchtime.

I kept thinking about Gwen and our dinner date the previous night. As I traversed the shoreline casting and retrieving my lure, I half-expected to see Chewie surface at any moment. Then I recalled that the small creek flowed into Stockade Lake, not Bismark.

Gwen hadn't messaged or texted me since I'd eaten dinner at her house and I wondered if I should call her. Instead, I texted her some phone pics of some of the fish I'd caught.

Eventually, I received the response: *Kewl catch. Clean them yourself.*

Well, at least she hasn't dropped off of the face of the Earth since last night.

After dad and I returned home, we cleaned the fish and took them inside to the kitchen to mom, who wanted to try some new style of breading on them for dinner that evening.

Not long after I unloaded our tackle and equipment

from the Blazer, I received a text message from Gwen.

Home yet?

Yep. Just got back, I replied.

Then nothing, so I went upstairs to my room to work on homework for both geometry and English. Even though I studied hard and received good grades, I still hated doing homework.

A couple of hours later, just before dinner, the doorbell rang.

"Scott, you have a visitor!" Mom yelled from downstairs.

As soon as I hit the bottom of the stairs, I spotted Gwen standing in the entryway holding a square plastic container.

Mom gave me a little smirk as she passed me on her way back toward the kitchen.

"Hi," Gwen offered with a small wave of her hand.

"Hey," I said. "Come on in."

"No, I really can't stay," she said. "I just wanted to drop these by for you."

"Oh," I said, somewhat disappointed.

I took the relatively large container from her and peeked inside at the numerous brownie squares. The aroma was so amazing that it made my mouth water.

"Wow, thanks," I said with an appreciative grin.

"You're welcome. I just wanted to make sure that you got these in time for dinner tonight," she said. "And I'm sorry that you missed out on dessert last night."

"Hey, no problem," I said.

"Well, I better get going," she said, turning to leave.

"I'll walk you out," I offered, setting the container on the edge of the small table next to our front door.

The sun had nearly set as I walked Gwen out to the driveway where her Suzuki SUV was parked.

"Are you doing okay?" I asked, following behind her as she walked to her vehicle.

"Sure, I'm fine," she said.

I reached out to wrap my arm around her waist, and rotated her body around until she was facing me. She seemed surprised and her wide eyes stared up into mine.

"Really," I insisted. "Is everything okay?"

Her small hands reached up to grasp my biceps as I pulled her closer to me.

"Fine," she said somewhat breathlessly.

"I really enjoyed yesterday at the pond," I offered. "And I'm really glad to see you today. Thanks for bringing the brownies to me, too. Did you make them?"

She nodded and said, "You're welcome. And yes, I made them myself, though they came from a box mix, so it's not scratch or anything."

My heart raced as I held her in my arms, relishing the feeling. I had strong feelings for her, and I was a little surprised by how much I'd missed her in such a short period of time.

"I enjoy spending time with you," I said. "And I hate to see you unhappy, like last night."

"I like our time together, too, Scott," she agreed. "And I'm sorry about last night. Mom just really upset me."

"You did seem pretty upset, but I think that I understand."

"No, you can't, really," she quietly disagreed. "But you're one of the first people to actually try and that means a lot to me."

She smiled back at me as I stared down into her beautiful blue eyes.

"In fact, you mean a lot to me," she added.

I drew my face closer to hers, intent on kissing her. We were so close that I felt her breath against my lips.

But at the last minute, she moved and rubbed her soft cheek against mine. Then she turned to press her lips against my cheek and kissed me there.

"I care about you, Scott, and I wouldn't ever want to hurt you," she whispered in my ear.

Then she released her grip on my arms and slid out of my grasp.

"But---" I protested as she opened the door to her SUV

and hopped inside.

"Sorry, I gotta' get back home," she said. "Enjoy the brownies."

I watched her drive off, feeling more confused than when she'd arrived. However, I definitely enjoyed how things had felt between us for at least a few moments.

After dinner, I knew that one thing was certain; Gwen knew how to make really great brownies.

* * *

At school on Wednesday afternoon, I checked in with the main office to let them know that I was leaving to attend my appointment with Dr. Webber, which Mom had arranged earlier that week.

Despite my mother being a nurse, I still had to sit in the waiting room like everybody else. The strange thing about visiting the hospital in a small town like Custer was that you invariably recognized most of the people there, except for the occasional tourists or visitors just passing through on their way to other attractions.

Soon after I arrived, Mom called me back to one of the examining rooms.

"Hi, Mom," I said as I walked past her to the examining rooms.

Once seated on the examining table, Mom checked my pulse and blood pressure.

"You could've just examined me this morning and told Dr. Webber how I was feeling, you know," I noted.

"No, I couldn't," she said with a reproving look.

As if perfectly timed, Dr. Webber strode into the room.

"Hello, Scott," she said in a pleasant, practiced manner. "How's my favorite safety today?"

"Ready for Friday's game," I confidently replied.

Mom shook her head at me.

"He's all yours, doctor," Mom said with a smirk. "I get enough of him at home."

"You're all heart, Mom," I chided.

She winked at me as she walked past me to exit the room, pulling the door shut behind her.

"Your mother is a wonderful nurse," Dr. Webber offered as she flashed a light into my eyes a few times.

"Yeah," I agreed. "She's a pretty cool mom, too. Just don't tell her that I said that."

"No problem. Doctor-patient confidentiality," she promised.

Dr. Webber examined my reflexes and balance and asked me questions about how I was feeling, including any unusual symptoms that I may have had.

In the end, she agreed that I was cleared to play in Friday's game against the Lead-Deadwood Golddiggers.

There sure are some strangely named teams in our region.

As Dr. Webber entered some note into an electronic tablet, she said, "Gwen certainly seems to be smitten with you, Scott."

I grinned despite myself.

"Yeah, I feel pretty much the same," I replied.

Dr. Webber briefly smiled up at me before returning to her notes.

"I appreciate how you've helped her to embrace being more social," she said. "Please, just bear in mind that Gwen's been through some traumatic experiences in recent years and she's still a sensitive young lady; not to mention the fact that you're the first boy that she's ever dated."

First dating aside, I wondered what she meant by 'sensitive.'

"My apologies," Dr. Webber added. "You're hardly a boy anymore, Scott, but rather a fit young man."

"Thank you," I said. "Please know that I'd never do anything to intentionally hurt Gwen."

She turned her attention fully on me.

"I appreciate that, Scott," she said. "You seem like a wonderful young man, and your mother is very proud of you. Jean seems to be a good judge of character, as well, so I'm hardly worried. However, I also know my daughter. Gwen might need some additional time to acclimate to more social circumstances, so I just wanted to encourage you to be patient with her, that's all."

I nodded and said, "Sure, I can do that."

"Thank you," she said, returning once more to her tablet.

"Dr. Webber, I am curious about something from Gwen's past," I prompted, to which she looked up at me with a curious expression.

"Yes?"

"Gwen's sort of left me with the impression that she doesn't trust herself around other people," I said. "Do you happen to know why she feels that way?"

Dr. Webber quietly considered me at length.

"Gwen has felt, and still feels, a great deal of guilt from the accident that took the lives of her father and brother," she said. "She feels as though she should have done more to help."

"But she was only twelve," I said. "And she was an accident victim, as well."

What more could a little girl have done under those circumstances?

"You're more right than you know," Dr. Webber alluded.

Something told me that there was an important insight in her statement, but I had no idea what that might be.

"I just don't know why she's so reluctant to be around other people," I said. "Some people at school talk about how she practically withdrew from everyone the day after the accident, and a number of her former friends have no idea why."

Dr. Webber sighed as switched off her tablet.

"Scott, you mean well, but there's still so much that you don't know, or understand, about Gwen and her past," she said.

"Then, why not help me to help her?" I asked. "I can't help her if I don't know what's wrong, and she certainly isn't talking to me about it."

"Please don't take what I'm about to say the wrong way, Scott. I've been diligently working with Gwen for years since the accident and you may have to come to terms with the fact that there are matters that you may not be well-equipped to confront or help her with," Dr. Webber explained. "But you've done a wonderful job just being her friend and spending time with her. You're helping in more ways than you may realize."

"For some reason, it's almost as if Gwen thinks that she's a danger to others," I blurted out. "Why is that?"

Dr. Webber fell silent again.

"Self-image is a powerful thing, Scott. We see ourselves quite differently from how others see us. Unfortunately, Gwen doesn't see herself in a particularly positive light," she said. "Gwen's a beautiful, talented, and intelligent young woman."

"She's very beautiful," I agreed. "And she's *definitely* smart; she runs circles around me in American Lit."

"Well, Gwen has been an avid reader for many years. In essence, she lives vicariously through the characters and stories that she reads about. She has socially sheltered herself from the real world, after all. Consider the fact that, until she started seeing you, her closest friends were a bulldog and a fully-grown alligator," Dr. Webber noted.

I had to admit that she made a good point there.

As I hopped down from the examining table and started to leave, Dr. Webber touched my shoulder, and said, "If you really do care about Gwen, just keep doing what you're doing. I'm hopeful that she'll open up more eventually."

"I will," I replied. "Thanks for the chat, Dr. Webber."

After chatting with Mom on the way out, I considered my conversation with Dr. Webber. Frankly, I felt very concerned about how Gwen saw herself.

Then I wondered what, if anything, Gwen's mother hadn't confided in me about her daughter.

CHAPTER 12

Lead-Deadwood was a town northwest of Rapid City, so it was quite a lengthy ride on the team bus Friday evening before we arrived at their high school. The Golddiggers, or Diggers as they were often called, were widely regarded as a formidable team in our league, but one that the Wildcats had been able to win against in previous seasons.

As such, their hometown crowd seemed to be particularly incensed about playing us. I felt as though our team had stepped into a hotly contested rivalry. Their maroon, white, and gold team colors were everywhere. And due to the significant distance separating our two schools, not as many of the typical Custer faithful made the trip with us, resulting in a quieter than usual cheering section for our team.

Still, our cheerleaders screamed and shouted their lungs out for us. Though Dr. Webber didn't make the trip, Mom, Dad, and Gwen were in the stands. My parents had rarely missed my games back in Springfield, and I was happy to see that they felt equally committed once we moved to Custer. And, of course, I was especially happy to see that Gwen made the trip, too.

Both our offense and defense played a great game, and we had a quick start from the opening kickoff. Our defense forced two turnovers and nabbed no less than four interceptions, one of which my good friend and fellow safety, Ben, scored a touchdown on. I managed one of the interceptions, but more importantly, broke up multiple passes and made some key tackles. Consequently, there were a number of three and outs for the Diggers offense.

The final score was a satisfying thirty-nine to three for us Wildcats. It was a great feeling to have near-complete control of a game on both sides of the ball, and gave us a great boost of confidence at the midpoint in the season. We were already on a three-game winning streak, having only lost our opening game against the More Cavaliers.

I was stoked over our prospects to finish out with a winning season.

But, as Dad always said, one game at a time.

After the game, I celebrated with the team on the bus ride home, but my mind kept wandering to my upcoming date with Gwen that Saturday evening.

I had to admit that, unlike other girls I'd dated, Gwen was definitely getting under my skin, but in a really good way.

* * *

I picked Gwen up from her house early on Saturday evening around five o'clock. She wore a black skirt made from a ruffled, light fabric and a black leather jacket worn over her purple top, which made her look both cute and edgy looking. Her dark hair was combed straight, casually falling about her face and shoulders.

"You look great," I said as we pulled out of her driveway.

"Thanks. So do you," she said as she hooked up her iPod to my stereo system. "I hope that you don't mind, but I'm providing the music tonight."

Now, Now's "Prehistoric" began to play.

"Sure," I replied.

We talked about music for a time as we traveled up the highway toward Rapid City. It was dark by the time we made it into town, and I pulled into the parking lot of a steak house called Oliver's Grill just off of I-90 that my dad had been telling me about recently.

The food was great. Gwen worked through her salad pretty quickly and watched me devour a big, thick steak for most of the time we were there. We chatted about school and movies.

Her entire face lit up as she recounted a funny story about how Dundee had chased her around the house after she snatched a dog chew from him earlier that day.

After dinner, we went to a place called Race Time, an indoor racing track hosting miniaturized racecars. However, instead of renting their normal racing cars, Gwen and I spent time on their outdoors bumper cars track. It was a blast, and Gwen laughed so hard that she frequently had trouble maneuvering her bumper cart.

Later, we grabbed some frozen yogurt and sat in my Blazer talking until it was almost ten-thirty. Then we headed back down the highway toward Custer.

We had had an awesome evening together.

After a quiet pause in our conversation, Lindsey Pavao's rendition of "Heart-Shaped Box" played on the stereo when I finally decided to take the chance to ask about something that had been preying on my mind all week.

"Gwen, would you get angry if I asked you to talk about something sensitive?" I asked.

She glanced sidelong at me with a guarded expression.

"Like what?"

"You're a really wonderful person, Gwen," I began. "You have a great sense of humor, and you're so smart. I just can't understand why you shut yourself away from everyone after the accident. I mean, I can imagine how hard that must have been for you, but why push everyone away?"

Gwen remained silent for a time.

"The accident was so horrible for me in so many ways; you just can't imagine how much. It changed me into someone that I didn't like anymore; somebody who I haven't liked since."

I patiently waited, hoping that she would say more. However, the silence only grew between us.

"I don't understand," I said while glancing over at her, completely confused.

"Look out!" Gwen screamed.

I looked up just in time to see a large animal lying in the middle of the road, and I slammed on my brakes just in time to avoid hitting it.

"Holy crap," I cursed and activated my hazard lights.

We both exited the blazer to see a large deer lying on the asphalt. While it was still alive, its breathing appeared labored.

It stared up at us with a wild-eyed look and suddenly sprang to its legs to run, only to fall down again onto the grass on the shoulder of the road.

I grabbed Gwen's arm, pulling her behind me, and we gingerly approached the animal. By the glow from my headlights, I could see blood coming from its nostrils and it appeared that at least one leg was broken.

"Poor thing must have been hit," said Gwen.

"Yeah, and not long ago," I added.

It was a horrible sight, and my mind raced for some sort of solution.

"What should we do? Should I call a veterinarian?" I asked.

Gwen sighed and slowly squatted down next to the poor animal.

"Be careful," I warned, moving closer to her.

She waved me off and shushed me.

"It's okay, boy," she cooed to the deer, placing her hand against its brown fur coat. "He's dying," she whispered.

I numbly stared down at Gwen.

"He's definitely in bad shape, but how do you know that?" I asked.

"Trust me. I know," she replied. "There's nothing we can do for him now, except maybe---"

"Maybe, what?" I asked, squatting down next to her.

"Shh," she urged.

I watched as she placed her other hand against the deer's shoulder. After a moment, its breathing grew shallower.

"Move back," she whispered harshly.

I stared at her dumbfounded as her hands gently pressed against the deer's body.

"Back!" she snapped, glaring up at me.

I stepped back just as I felt a wave of nausea wash through my body. Then a sense of light-headedness and weakness swept through me and I nearly lost my breath.

A moment later, the deer exhaled a final, large breath and then fell silent. The deer's eyes closed and it almost looked peaceful as it lay still on the ground.

It was about that time that my strength returned, as if nothing had happened.

Gwen inhaled a large breath and then let it out slowly before rising to stand. As she turned toward me, I thought that I saw a small, fleeting twinkle in her eyes.

"Are you okay?" I asked.

"I'm fine," she said curtly.

I looked back down at the deer and noticed something strange. All of the grass within three or four feet of the deer had suddenly turned brown, almost dormant-looking. But I was certain that it had been green grass only moments prior.

"What happened to the grass?"

"Nothing," Gwen quickly replied. "It was like that already."

"No," I said. "I'm pretty sure that it wasn't."

"It doesn't matter, Scott," she said somewhat defensively.

"Hey, I'm not trying to argue with you or anything," I said.

What's gotten into her all of the sudden? More to the point, what did she do to that deer?

"Please, just take me home," she insisted. "I don't want to be here any longer."

Before I could say anything further, she'd already run to the passenger side of my Blazer and hopped into the cab.

I shook my head as I hurried into the driver's seat.

We hadn't proceeded up the road more than a hundred feet when I saw a truck's tail lights flashing on the eastern side of the highway. I could see wavy, black skid marks leading off the road, and the truck was lodged against a large tree approximately twenty feet from the pavement.

"Look at that," I said, slowing down to gain a clearer view.

"What?" Gwen asked.

"I think somebody crashed their truck," I replied.

I pulled over onto the highway's shoulder and activated my hazard lights again. Then, I reached under my seat and pulled out my large-beam flashlight.

"Stay here," I ordered.

"The hell I will," she retorted.

"Well, stay close to me," I insisted. "And call 911."

We both exited the Blazer, but a northbound car was coming toward us at a high rate of speed, so I made sure that we remained on our side of the road. I thought that it might stop, but it sped right past us.

"C'mon," I said, hurrying toward the crashed vehicle.

"My phone's not getting any signal here," Gwen said.

I checked my phone which also had no connection.

Wonderful. So much for national cellular coverage.

I shined my light onto the truck, which had smoke and steam coming out from underneath the hood where it had impacted the huge tree.

As I made my way around to the driver's side, I heard moaning. After I managed to dislodge the driver's side door by sheer force, it slowly creaked open.

I saw a middle-aged woman pinned back against the driver's seat by a broken tree limb that had penetrated the windshield and impaled her to the chest.

She was semi-conscious and beginning to rouse. A bearded man seated next to her was draped over the dashboard, and was either dead or merely unconscious.

"My God, this is bad," I muttered as the strong smell of alcohol permeated the air inside the cab.

To say that it was a horrible situation was the understatement of the year.

"Oh, no," Gwen gasped from behind me. "Not again."

I looked back at her and saw her horrified expression.

Then the woman woke and started both screaming and crying.

"Just stay calm," I urged, though I felt like a complete idiot.

My mind felt numb as I struggled to find a way to remove the branch. Then I realized that what we really needed was the fire department.

"See if you can flag down somebody," I said to Gwen over the woman's painful cries.

"It's too late," she said. "She's already dying."

I looked up at Gwen as if she was insane.

How could she possibly know that?

"What?" I demanded.

The man in the passenger seat groaned and began to move.

"Mister, just stay put," I said. "You might be injured."

The man's eyes flickered open and immediately focused upon the crying woman.

"Sally! Oh no, Sally," he bellowed in an anguished voice.

The situation was completely out of hand and I had absolutely no idea what to do at that moment.

I felt Gwen's hand grasp my shoulder from behind and she pulled at me.

"Move, Scott!" she ordered.

Then I remembered the deer.

"Hold on," I urged, reaching for her hand.

"For God's sake, do something! Help her!" the man screamed at me as his shaking hands tried to pull at the branch.

The woman's screams were ear-shattering.

"I can ease her pain," Gwen pleaded.

"Wait, we can try to cut the limb free or something," I insisted.

The woman screamed in agony in a manner that sent a cold chill down my spine.

"Dammit, let this girl help, Sally!" the man yelled. "Hold on, Sally, hold on."

"P-please help," the woman managed to mutter before returning to a fit of gasping.

"Scott, move," Gwen pleaded in my ear. "She's suffering; can't you hear her?"

I stared at her as if I didn't even recognize her.

Just what was she trying to do, anyway?

I heard the heavy squealing of air brakes back at the highway and I stepped away from the vehicle to see a semi-tractor trailer stopped alongside the road.

"Ya'll need some help?" Came a gruff man's voice.

"Yeah!" I shouted. "We got a woman pinned in here!"

"Stay put! I'll get on the radio!" yelled the man.

Thank God, for truck drivers.

When I turned back to Gwen, she was already leaning inside the cab.

"She's in so much pain," Gwen whispered harshly.

"Gwen, wait!" I urged.

The woman continued to wail in a terrible manner, each scream sending a fresh chill down my spine.

"Just do whatever you gotta' do!" the man yelled.

"I can only help to comfort her; ease her pain," Gwen insisted. "Nothing more."

Then I heard the sound of the woman's cries subside, and she moaned, "Can't stand this anymore...go ahead, girly."

I thought that I heard Gwen whisper, "I'm so sorry."

"Love...you...Lester," the woman whispered.

I reached out to grab Gwen by the arm to try to stop her, but she yelled, "Get back, Scott!"

Then she reared back her leg and kicked me squarely in

the stomach with the heel of her foot, knocking me backward and slightly off-balance.

In the second that it took to right myself, I felt a wave of nausea pass through my stomach, just like what happened with the deer.

A second later, I felt slightly dizzy.

"What the hell—" the man gasped as he slumped back against the seat.

A moment later, Gwen stepped back from the cab and sat down hard onto the ground.

I rushed to her side, but she just stared blankly back at me. Once again, I thought that I saw a brief twinkle in her blue eyes.

Then it was gone.

"Sally? Sally!" the man shouted.

"There was nothing else I could do for her," Gwen mumbled. "It's all that I could ever do."

Then she started crying.

I tried to grasp the meaning behind what she just said, but the pieces weren't falling into place for me.

"She's dead!" the man yelled. "Damn you! What the hell did you do to her, girl!"

Oh, crap.

The situation was turning uglier, as if it were even possible.

The man staggered outside of the truck. He was cursing as he rounded the backside of the vehicle coming toward us.

"I called the authorities," said the truck driver as he approached us. "They're on the way."

"You freak! You killed her!" seethed the man.

I charged forward to meet him before he got anywhere near Gwen.

"Whoa, calm down, Mister!" demanded the truck driver as the angry man rushed me.

"Hey, back off," I growled.

The man was a bearded, middle-aged fellow who looked like the kind of guy you met in a biker bar somewhere; and not the friendly type. He balled up his fists, though he seemed to have trouble standing up straight.

He had to be drunk.

As he barreled toward me, I slammed him in the chest with the flat of one hand, knocking him to the ground.

"Back off, man!" I ordered.

It made me angry that we had only tried to help, even though I didn't know what to think about Gwen's actions.

One thing was certain; I was in no mood to put up with some drunken guy punching on me, personal trauma or not.

All that I wanted was for help to arrive so that I could concentrate on supporting Gwen.

"Hey, just calm down, old feller," cautioned the truck driver. "Everybody here's just trying to help out."

"The lady driving the truck just died," I said, pointing back to the cab.

"Aw, hell," muttered the truck driver grimly.

Then I heard sirens in the distance.

"Ain't nobody died!" The man yelled with slurred speech. "That witch over there killed her!"

"Now, now, just take it easy," insisted the truck driver. "Nobody killed anybody; this is just a bad accident."

Then the man broke down and started crying and cursing.

I returned my attention to Gwen to see her rubbing at her eyes.

"See? I'm cursed, Scott," she whispered harshly between sobs. "I tried to tell you, but you wouldn't listen. I'm damaged."

"No, you're not," I reassured her as I knelt beside her and held her in my arms as the authorities arrived on scene.

Then a thought struck me, and I reached next to myself to pick up my flashlight. Shining the light near the driver's side door of the truck, I noticed a circular patch of dead grass and weeds where Gwen had been standing when the woman had died.

But I was too stunned and concerned over Gwen's well-being to ponder the implications any further.

CHAPTER 13

I leaned back against the county sheriff's patrol car with one arm around Gwen's shoulders as the deputy sheriff and a highway patrolman asked us details about the accident. I told him about us finding the dying deer and then coming upon the crashed truck.

"It looks like that truck must have hit the deer and then veered further down the highway and across the oncoming lane until impacting the tree," said the deputy to the patrolman. "The deer frequently run across the country roads and highways around here. It didn't help that alcohol was involved, either."

"It's a bad situation, for certain." The highway patrolman agreed with a nod.

He spared a glance at Gwen and me, and then walked over to the crash scene to help direct a tow truck driver who was backing up his rig.

Gwen remained relatively silent during the remainder of the interview, only briefly answering questions when asked. It was as if she had retreated into herself or something.

At any rate, it really worried me.

"And you two were returning from where, exactly?" asked the deputy.

"Rapid City," I replied. "We had gone out for dinner and

then bumper cars."

The deputy turned his attention back to Gwen.

"The passenger in the truck, Lester Newcomb, claims that you had something to do with the death of the injured woman who had been driving," he said. "Based upon what I saw, I don't see how that's possible, myself, but perhaps you could tell me your side of the story."

Gwen dully explained, "I tried to calm her and the man demanded that I do something. In the end, I only said that I could help to comfort her. So, that's what I did."

The deputy scribbled some notes and then studied Gwen's driver's license at length.

"By any chance, are you Dr. Olivia Webber's daughter?" he asked.

"Yes," she replied.

The deputy took a long look at her and said, "I thought so. Gwen, I was one of the officers that responded to the accident that claimed your father and brother a few years ago. I'm really sorry that you were here to have to see this tonight."

Gwen nodded and leaned her head back against my shoulder.

The deputy turned his attention to me.

"Do you feel okay to drive or would you like for me to call your parents?"

"I'm okay, sir," I replied.

"Why don't you go ahead and take her home, son," the deputy suggested. "We can call you both sometime later if we have additional questions."

"Yes, sir," I replied.

I held my arm around Gwen supportively as we walked back to my truck. We didn't say a word to each other on the way back to her house, but then, I wasn't sure what I could have said to her at that moment. What we had just experienced was shocking, and there were just too many other variables running through my head.

I managed to call Gwen's mother just a few miles further

down the road, though the signal on my phone was weak. Nevertheless, I'd been able to tell her the basics of what had happened. Then I called my parents.

Dr. Webber was waiting in the driveway for us as I pulled up and she immediately moved to open the passenger side door.

Gwen practically leapt from the truck into her mother's arms amidst a fresh barrage of tears.

I got out of the truck and made my way around to where Gwen and her mother stood.

"It's okay now, my dear," Dr. Webber said soothingly. "It's all over."

"It happened," Gwen vaguely whispered.

Feeling both helpless and useless, I stuck my palms into the back pockets of my jeans and just stood there.

"Thank you, Scott," Dr. Webber offered. "I'll take care of her from here."

I nodded, shut the passenger door, and numbly made my way back into the Blazer. My short drive home felt surreal after what had happened.

Mom and Dad were up waiting for me and they had a host of questions about what had happened. Like me, they were shocked by what Gwen and I had encountered on that dark stretch of state highway.

It was well after two o'clock that morning before I finally crawled into bed. Unfortunately, the night's events kept replaying in my mind like a bad nightmare.

I felt so sorry for the poor woman who had died, as well as concerned for what Gwen had gone through.

I wasn't certain what exactly Gwen had done to the deer and the woman, but I had a suspicion. Though, while unnerving, and despite what that man had accused, it didn't seem particularly evil.

What had Gwen called it?

A curse.

* * *

I woke up with a start from a deep sleep to discover that it was well past ten o'clock in the morning. I checked my phone but saw no messages from Gwen, so I sent her a text message to see how she was doing.

By the time that I'd finished showering and dressing, there was still no response from her. After calling her cell phone and getting no response, I tried her home number.

"Hello?" answered Gwen's mother.

"Hi, Dr. Webber. I was just calling to speak with Gwen," I said.

"Just a moment, Scott."

After a few moments of silence, Dr. Webber returned to say, "I'm sorry, Scott, but Gwen's not feeling up to visiting right now. I'll be sure to tell her that you called, though."

I thanked her and sat on the edge of my bed wondering why Gwen wouldn't speak to me.

Once downstairs, Mom and Dad asked how I was doing as I ate brunch. When I told them about my failed attempt to speak to Gwen, they tried reassuring me.

"I can only imagine how traumatic that must have been for her, given what she experienced just years prior," Mom ventured. "It must have brought back a lot of troubling memories and feelings for her. Give her a little time. She'll come around eventually."

I conceded that mom might have been correct, but it still bothered me. Of course, I had little time to consider the matter further because Dad asked me to accompany him to the grocery store to help with some inventory. While it helped me pass the time, it hardly made me forget about either Gwen or what we'd experienced together the night before.

By late Sunday afternoon, I decided to try and formulate my own answers. I drove out to the stretch of Highway 16 where the accident had occurred.

I first stopped at the location where the truck had impacted the tall oak tree. In the absence of the pickup or victims, the only signs of anything untoward were the tire marks leading off the road, some broken glass, and the subsequent indentions on the ground.

The larger tree was relatively damaged and might have to be cut down. A smaller evergreen tree that had originally eluded me that night was lying not far away; its four-inch diameter trunk was snapped in half.

Then I noticed the circular patch of dead grass and weeds where Gwen had been standing. I stepped upon the grass and it crunched beneath my feet.

"Weird," I said.

I walked across the highway and up further where we had found the dying deer. A dried bloodstain marked the spot on the highway where the poor animal had originally lain. Then I noticed another dead patch of grass, along with another area of dried blood, alongside the highway's shoulder.

Once again, the grass was so dry that it crunched beneath my feet.

"How did Gwen do that?" I asked aloud.

More to the point, what kind of ability existed that could do that? Magic?

Maybe it was some ability that was divinely granted; or perhaps something darker and less-than-divine.

Gwen seemed like such a kind, sweet person that I had a hard time imagining that what had happened could have anything to do with something dark or evil.

Then I glanced down at the dead grass again.

In two separate instances, living beings and grass had died that night as a result of Gwen's intervention.

But what was I supposed to do next?

* * *

I slept poorly Sunday night, tossing and turning for what felt like endless hours. My mind just wouldn't turn itself off; my thoughts kept returning to Gwen and the accident.

When I finally did fall asleep, I had a weird dream about

Gwen and me walking hand-in-hand across football fields of brown, lifeless turf. Occasionally, there was a variety of dead animals lying interspersed along the sidelines.

I awoke in a cold sweat only ten minutes prior to my alarm going off.

All day Monday, Gwen didn't return either my calls or text messages, and it bothered me to no end. It'd been hard for me to concentrate on my classes that day.

Of course, everyone had heard about Saturday night's accident. Throughout the day, a host of friends and classmates grilled me over what had happened. I was careful not to reveal anything about Gwen or her role in the accident, including her influence over the deer. Fortunately, the actual event at its base level was more than interesting enough for everyone.

Someone had died, and they found it interesting.

It struck me as odd. But then, would I have been any less interested in hearing about what had happened if it had been someone else who'd been there instead of me?

My grandmother and dad's catch phrase returned.

Life was definitely fickle.

Then my mind reflected on Gwen. I hoped that she was doing okay.

During football practice on Monday afternoon, I only did the minimum workout required before heading home to check my email and Facebook messages.

Still no response from Gwen.

Tuesday went much the same as Monday, and I did a horrible job on my homework assignments.

When I called Gwen's house, her mother assured me that she was doing okay and once again suggested that Gwen would come around when she was ready to talk.

By Wednesday, and yet more continued silence from Gwen, I decided to take matters into my own hands. I felt that I had been very patient, and all that I wanted to do was make sure she was okay.

No girl in my life had ever had the kind of effect on me

that Gwen had, and I was at a loss to explain it. I just really, really liked her.

I was crushing on her something fierce. I just had to see her; talk to her.

That afternoon, formal football practice had been cancelled due to an administration and all-faculty meeting early that evening, and for the first time that I could recall, I wasn't particularly disappointed. Instead of either hanging out with my teammates and friends or going home after school as I normally might have done, I drove directly over to Gwen's house.

I was determined to see her, no matter what.

When I arrived at her house, I didn't see her SUV parked in the driveway. However, that didn't deter me, as I wagered that it must have been parked in one of the bays of their large three-car garage.

After I rang the doorbell, I heard Dundee barking inside. When Gwen's mother answered the door with a welcoming expression, I hoped that conditions had improved in the Webber household.

"Hello, Scott," she politely greeted.

"Hi, Dr. Webber," I offered. "I apologize for just stopping by unannounced, but I really need to see Gwen."

"Is everything okay?" she asked.

"I realize that things have been sort of strained between Gwen and me, but I think it's important that she and I talk things out," I explained.

"This is about the night of the accident, isn't it?"

I directly stared into her eyes, wondering if I could risk talking to her about the topic that had been preying on my mind.

Then again, I was almost certain that she already knew full well what I intended to ask Gwen about.

"Dr. Webber, I respect Gwen's privacy, but I deeply care about her, and I just need to know the truth about what's going on," I said.

She shook her head and sighed.

"I don't suppose that it would do any good to ask for you to just try and forget about the topic, would it?" she asked.

"Probably not," I admitted.

She frowned, as if debating whether to send me away or not.

"Listen, Dr. Webber, I haven't talked to *anyone* about what I really saw that night with Gwen," I insisted. "I've kept Gwen's secret, including from my parents, and will continue to do so. I just want to understand her better. How can I help her, if I don't even know the truth?"

The protracted, awkward silence that followed was unnerving.

"All right," she said. "Normally, I wouldn't feel comfortable that you've withheld information from your parents, but in this case, I'm afraid that it's probably for the best. Come in, and please try to keep an open mind."

"I will," I agreed with a nod.

I stepped inside and reached down to pet Dundee as the front door closed behind me. The bulldog happily wagged his stub of a tail and sniffed at my hand.

"Hey, boy," I greeted.

"He missed you, it seems," Dr. Webber observed.

"Hopefully, he's not the only one," I alluded.

"I'd be lying if I said that your absence has been easy on Gwen," she said.

"I'm glad that I'm not easy to forget," I said with a grin.

"Won't you have a seat in the living room?" she suggested, leading the way. "Would you like something to drink? I have iced tea already made and there are cold Cokes in the fridge."

"Thanks," I replied as I sat on the couch. "A Coke would be great."

A couple of moments later, she handed the soda can to me, already opened.

"Thank you," I said.

She perched on the edge of the recliner across from me.

"Um, is Gwen back in her room?" I asked, reaching

down to pet Dundee as he leaned against my leg wagging his tail.

"I'm afraid that she's not here right now," she replied. "Gwen went into town to run some errands about twenty minutes ago."

I frowned, wishing that I had made it over just a little sooner.

"But maybe it's better for just you and me to have a chat before she returns," she said.

"Okay," I said, taking a swig of soda.

"I've mentioned before that Gwen is a very sensitive girl," she began. "There I go again. She's a young lady now, I suppose; though she'll always feel like my little girl. Maybe that's one reason why I'm particularly protective over her; though there's really more to it than that."

I patiently waited for her to continue.

"Scott, tell me something," she carefully prefaced. "You mentioned a few moments ago that you want to know what's going on. What is it that you have questions about, exactly?"

"Well, I don't know what Gwen told you, but she did *something* to both the deer and the woman in the pickup that night," I replied. "I know that the things we saw that night were horrible; like nothing I'd ever seen firsthand, anyway. But Gwen seemed more upset about what she did than anything about the deer or the accident."

"And how do *you* feel about what she did?" Dr. Webber asked.

Her question caught me off guard. Of all of the things that I had been ready to talk about that afternoon, that certainly wasn't one of them.

"Well, I haven't really thought about that," I admitted. "But I don't think that Gwen did anything *wrong*, that's for certain. Heck, I'm not even sure what *that* was exactly."

"Did you happen to mention anything to the authorities about what Gwen may have done that night?"

"No, of course not," I insisted. "I told you, I haven't even talked to my parents about that."

Dr. Webber appeared very relieved.

"Thank you, Scott," she offered. "I'm very happy to hear you say that; more than you could know, actually."

I stared directly into her eyes.

"Dr. Webber, I haven't felt about anyone else before like I feel about Gwen," I said. "There isn't anything that I wouldn't do to help her. And I have no intention of telling anyone else about what I saw. If anything, it would only stir up more trouble for her reputation than what's already occurred around town."

"You seem to grasp the situation much better than I had expected, Scott," she sagely observed.

"Well, then, maybe you'd be willing to trust me enough to explain to me what it is that we're talking about," I said.

She quietly considered me at some length as I took another drink of Coke to assuage my fidgeting.

"My maiden name is Young and I'm descended from a long lineage that goes back to England's earliest history; though there are also ties through Europe, as well. The American side of my family's heritage dates back to the 1600s in what was then the English royal colony of Massachusetts," she said.

"Cool."

I had never thought to see how far back my own family's history went, though Grandma Blackstone used to tell stories about her side of the family when I was a kid. The truth was that I never found it that interesting, so I never paid close attention.

"Have you ever heard of the Salem witch trials?" Dr. Webber asked.

"Yeah, I remember them being mentioned in one of my history classes," I replied. "Though I don't recall much about them, really."

Then it struck me what she was getting at.

"Wait, is Gwen a *witch*?" I demanded.

Dundee barked beside me.

"*Be calm*," Dr. Webber encouraged as she held up her

hand for silence and looked down at Dundee, who quietly lay back down onto the carpet next to me.

I felt a soothing wave course through me.

"Let's just step back for a moment," she cautioned. "We're not talking about real witches here, Scott. And, no, Gwen is most assuredly not a witch. Of course, neither am I, for that matter."

I took a deep breath and sat my soda can on a coaster on the coffee table in front of me.

"You had me going there for a minute, Doc," I said, somewhat relieved.

"Some members of my family line are what you might call Reapers," she calmly explained as she placed her hands in her lap.

I looked at her in shock.

"Reapers?" I asked. "Like the *Grim Reaper*?"

She pleasantly smiled.

"Well, there is no actual Grim Reaper," she replied. "The Grim Reaper is nothing more than a fictional character dating back as far as the fifteenth century. He's a personification of death in stories, for the most part. Although there are references to a being called Death dating back to the Hellenic Period in Ancient Greece."

I was stunned, to say the least.

"You seem to know a lot about the Grim Reaper," I noted. "You sound like a Wikipedia entry."

"The distinctions between reality and legend are particularly important where my family lineage is concerned," she said. "The research stretches back many generations. My mother lectured me on such things when I was just a girl. Gwen is already as well-versed as I am."

"And you and Gwen are both---" I slowly said.

"Reapers," she replied matter-of-factly. "We have the ability to influence the life force of living things."

My heart pounded as I contemplated what she was telling me. I thought back to the dead patch of grass that surrounded the deer and the area where Gwen had been standing near the truck.

"So, you both can kill living things," I said. "You take souls?"

Dr. Webber frowned.

"No, we don't take souls," she said. "The soul is an essence that Reapers have no sway or influence over. However, the life force is something different altogether."

"In the strictest sense, yes, we have the ability to kill living things. But you're only focusing on the negative aspects of that topic," she gently admonished. "A Reaper's body can absorb the life forces, or energies, from any living things, as well as transfer and channel, or even bring balance to those energies. Look at the plants around you, for example."

I scanned the living room, noting the litany of flowers and houseplants I'd noticed from the very first time that I set foot in the Webber house. They were vibrant-looking.

"They are very much alive and well, are they not?" she asked.

I nodded. "Yeah, actually," I replied. "You should open a florist shop or a greenhouse."

The edge of her mouth upturned slightly.

"Well, that's because I helped to nurture the life force of the plants by balancing out their respective growths, taking small amounts of energy from some to assist others," she explained. "The same can be done with animals or people. That's why I chose to be a physician—to *help* people."

I considered the surrounding plants once more.

"You know, Gwen said before that she's not very good with plants," I recalled.

"And now we're getting to the heart of the matter," Gwen's mother said. "Gwen's not very good with balancing life forces. In fact, she's what I think of as a magnet; she can absorb life force, but has trouble rechanneling it."

"So, she can only kill, then?" I asked.

That was a really creepy prospect. However, Gwen seemed like such a kind, gentle person; definitely not the killer type.

Dr. Webber sighed.

"At least, she only thinks that she can," she replied. "However, in the case of both the deer and the poor woman that you encountered, Gwen actually provided them with comfort in their final moments. In essence, she performed acts of mercy under regrettably fatal circumstances."

I frowned. "Have you done that for people?" I carefully asked.

"On occasion," she gently replied. "When humane circumstances warranted it, though with a patient's consent, when possible. I try to live by the physician's creed, *Thou shalt do no harm.*"

I nodded as I digested that tidbit of information, though I noticed a peculiar expression on Dr. Webber's face.

"But?" I asked.

"Well, in limited cases, I also feel that people reap what they sow, so to speak," she said.

I didn't think that I'd ever think of that term in quite the same way again. Still, Gwen's mother seemed like a kind person, as well as a competent physician.

"I don't think that Gwen sees the whole 'mercy perspective' in the same way that you do. The other night, she said that she was cursed," I recalled.

"She only *thinks* that she's cursed, so she created a mental block about herself and her abilities," Dr. Webber clarified. "This is precisely what I've been trying to remediate in her since she was twelve; since the days following the accident. But she keeps fighting me. No, she keeps fighting herself, remaining in a state of perpetual denial and self-loathing."

The passion in her voice was almost ominous.

"Gwen hates herself?" I asked.

"I'm afraid that's part of it," she replied. "Gwen blames herself for the death of her little brother, Tommy, for example."

"What? Why?"

Her face took on a pained expression.

"On the night of the accident that claimed my husband

and son's lives five years ago, Gwen had only just turned twelve and discovered that her own powers were manifesting. The Reaper abilities only manifest themselves in select branches of my family's bloodline, as it had with my mother and me. Barely a month following Gwen's birthday, she confided in me that she had been able to feel life forces."

"When I began tutoring her in some early exercises, I found that she was exceptionally adept at absorbing life forces, but not skilled at either returning them or rebalancing them into other living organisms," she continued. "We started with small plants and insects, but she didn't seem to be able to grasp the skill for rechanneling. It upset her tremendously."

"Then the accident occurred," she sadly recalled. "Initially, she was near-catatonic, and nearly two weeks passed before she finally spoke to anyone. Eventually, she reached the point where she was willing to discuss the accident, including what had ensued before emergency responders arrived."

"What happened?" I asked.

"Gwen said that she could sense that her father had already died immediately following the crash, but she still sensed Tommy's fading strength. With no degree of expertise and minimal amounts of cursory mentoring to draw upon, she desperately tried to channel some of her life force into Tommy. Instead, she said that her body kept absorbing his strength rather than giving her own. Soon afterward, Tommy quickly succumbed to his injuries. It must have been a horrific experience for her."

"So, Gwen didn't actually kill Tommy, then?" I asked.

Dr. Webber inhaled deeply and slowly let her breath out before speaking.

"No, I don't think so," she said. "Tommy's brain had experienced internal hemorrhaging. It appeared that, following the initial impact, his head had slammed against the car's side window with terrible force; enough to break the tempered glass."

"I'm so sorry," I said. "That's horrible beyond words."
I didn't know what else that I could say.

She regarded me with sad eyes that caused a tight feeling
in my chest. It was terrible enough seeing a stranger die in an
accident, that I couldn't imagine the anguish of losing
someone close to me that way.

"Despite my attempts to comfort Gwen and convince her
that she could have done so little to help her brother, her
guilt only grew from that time," Dr. Webber continued. "She
felt that she had failed not only her brother, but me as well,
though I tried to reassure her that it wasn't the case. She said
that she only knew how to kill."

"That's terrible," I said.

"Gwen cut herself off from those around her and she
refused to return to school, though at least she agreed to
home-schooling after a time. Ever since then, she's remained
reclusive; trapped in her guilt with only me, our pets, and an
alligator for company."

I shook my head.

"I don't understand," I said. "How is it that some of the
people around town could be so standoffish toward her?
There are some outlandish rumors and comments circulating
about her around the school, for example. Some people look
at her as if she's a freak or something."

One of Dr. Webber's brows arched.

"Indeed," she said. "Yet, I can recount from my own
family's history that people often fear, or turn to hate, both
people and things that they don't fully understand. Although,
I can't lay the blame on them entirely. They didn't, in fact
couldn't, know the full truth about what had really happened
in the accident."

"Come to think of it, I remember hearing someone in
town mention that they thought that Gwen had more to do
with the accident than what was known," I absently recalled.

"Really? That's troubling, to say the least," she said.
"Although it's hardly surprising how people's imaginations
can spin the most outlandish of suspicions over lack of

evidence and understanding."

"Gwen's so much more mature now," I ventured. "Can't you help her to balance her...skills?"

Dr. Webber shrugged. "Even today, Gwen refuses to practice and hone her Reaper talents because she's too scared to risk hurting another living thing."

I sat quietly, allowing the silence to grow between us as I contemplated everything that I'd just learned about Gwen and her tragic past.

But what could I do? I didn't have the slightest idea of what I could offer to help her.

"I appreciate you caring enough about Gwen to try and understand more about her, Scott," Dr. Webber offered. "And I realize how bizarre and surprising much of what I have told you must sound, but I must ask that you continue to keep this a secret between us. And regrettably, at least for the time being, I have to ask that you not speak to your parents about this, either. I have the highest respect for your mother, in particular, but this is a topic that needs to be delicately broached."

It made sense, really. Besides, who would believe me anyway?

"Sure," I replied.

"Can you imagine the kind of pandemonium that would erupt in town if word about Gwen and me got out?" she asked.

She made an excellent point.

"It would be the Salem witch trials all over again," she added. "My ancestor, Anne Young, was a midwife. She helped people, including birthing a host of children into this world. And yet, merely because of people's lack of understanding and their dogmatic beliefs, she and other innocent people were executed."

That thought was shocking. I couldn't let anything like that happen to either Gwen or her mother.

Ever.

"I completely understand," I replied. "You can count on me, Dr. Webber."

She regarded me with an expression of approval.

"You're a remarkable young man, Scott," she said. "I'm very happy that my daughter has met someone like you. You remind me somewhat of my late husband, Frank. He maintained an open mind as he came to understand me and my family's legacy. And still, he accepted me for who I was, and we had two beautiful children together. I still miss him so very much."

She abruptly stopped talking and I saw her eyes begin to glisten.

The front door abruptly opened and Gwen stood with a guarded expression, holding a grocery sack in each arm.

Dundee barked and raced to the door as I likewise rose to make my way toward her. I reached out to take both sacks from her.

"Hey, stranger," I muttered.

"Are you here to break up with me?" she asked in a small voice.

I chuckled. "Are you kidding? I came here to finally track you down," I replied.

Wordlessly, she gently encircled my waist with her arms and hugged her body against mine, pressing her head against my chest.

"I've really missed you," she whispered.

I grinned like a Cheshire cat.

"Well, Scott, I hope this means that you might join us for dinner tonight," Dr. Webber said.

"I wouldn't miss it for the world," I replied.

And though it felt kind of lame, I nevertheless called Mom to inquire if she or Dad had plans for me that evening. Fortunately, I was in the clear.

As I sat at the kitchen table watching Gwen and her mother preparing dinner, my mind considered everything that I'd learned about Gwen's past, including her mysterious family heritage.

"Somebody's deep in thought," Gwen observed as she sliced vegetables for a salad.

"I was just thinking about---" I started to say.

"Scott and I had a wonderful chat before you arrived this evening," Gwen's mother interrupted.

Gwen suspiciously looked at her mother and said, "Really. What kind of chat?"

"I told him a little about our family heritage," she said while stirring a pot on the stove. "I'm pleased to say that Scott was highly supportive and understanding."

"You told him about *us*?" she incredulously demanded.

"Yes, as a matter of fact, I did," she replied.

Gwen stared wide-eyed at me as I rose from the table to walk over to her.

"And you're still here?" she asked.

I stared down into her eyes as she stood before me.

"I'm not going anywhere," I slowly sounded out each word. "And you can't chase me away."

"You're seriously not even a little scared?"

"Your family's history isn't anything that would scare me away, Gwen," I insisted, taking the sharp knife from her and continuing to cut up the vegetables that she had started. "Move over and let a pro do this, or we'll never eat tonight. I'm hungry."

Somehow, I didn't think that it was good idea for Gwen to be around sharp knives if she suddenly turned emotional over the topic. Already, my protective nature for her was kicking into action.

She poked me on the shoulder with the tip of her sharp-nailed finger, and demanded, "What did she say about me? You need to tell me everything that she told you."

"There's time enough for that later," Gwen's mother insisted. "For now, let's finish getting dinner ready."

We returned to dinner preparations, and Gwen distractedly arranged plates and flatware on the table as she kept glancing over at me.

"You heard about our *entire* family legacy?" she asked.

I continued chopping red and green bell peppers before me.

"A proud family legacy, I'm told," I replied.

"Proud and tragic," Gwen clarified.

"We have a long line of doctors, nurses, midwives, and caregivers in our family heritage," Gwen's mother said. "And I'm proud to say that there are no bandits or evildoers that I know of."

"There are bad Reapers?" I asked, suddenly surprised that I hadn't considered that idea yet.

"Just me," Gwen muttered.

I glanced sidelong at her.

"There are no bad Reapers in *this* family," Dr. Webber sternly emphasized. "Just ones who have given up on their training," she reprovingly added.

Gwen folded her arms before her and glared back at her mother.

"Hey, no arguing," I suggested. "Hungry guest here."

Gwen struggled not to smirk but quickly failed. She took a nearby hand towel and swatted me with it.

"I'm all about practice," I said.

"Oh, shut up," she chided.

"Hey, if I don't go to football practice, how do you expect me to catch those interceptions and make the game-saving tackles?" I asked and looked over at Gwen's mother, who had adopted a pleased expression.

"This isn't a game," Gwen said.

"No, it isn't," I agreed. "It's life, and that makes it even more important."

Gwen growled and swatted me with the towel again. Mild stinging aside, it was nice to see her lightening up a little bit.

"Oh, just like you to turn all logical with me all of the sudden," she said.

"Hey, I'm pretty intelligent for a football player," I said with a shrug.

Gwen's mother laughed. "I think that he's a real keeper, Gwen," she offered.

"Too bad for you, he's already taken," she teased.

Then she sighed and lightly wrapped her arms around my

midsection, and I felt the side of her face press against my back.

"Okay, Scott. So, I suppose that maybe I'll consider trying some small exercises again sometime soon," she quietly conceded.

I nodded. To me, that sounded like a remarkable step forward given all that had happened recently.

CHAPTER 14

Having had an amazing, insightful conversation with Gwen's mother the night before, as well as spending quality time with Gwen, had definitely improved my mood by Wednesday morning. Part of that had to be that I finally got a decent night's sleep for the first time in days. Most importantly, I once again felt on a more stable footing regarding my relationship with Gwen.

Relationship.

Just the thought of that word combined with the vision of Gwen made me feel unusually happy inside. The experience from the truck accident of the past Friday was still prevalent in my mind, but somehow I was beginning to be able to deal with what had happened a little bit easier. Maybe part of that was having some understanding about Gwen and her role in the troubling events.

I'm having a relationship with a Reaper.

How cool is that?

"You look like you're in a trance," Mom quipped as she poured a cup of coffee. "Get enough sleep last night?"

I started, not having realized she'd wandered into the kitchen.

"Yeah, I'm good," I hastily replied before picking up my cereal bowl to drink the pool of milk that remained.

My eyes were drawn to the clock above the sink.

"Dang it, gotta' run," I said before grabbing my backpack and heading for the front door.

I was already running late so I'd have to brush my teeth later.

At any rate, I was in a pretty good mood for most of the morning. That was until lunchtime, at least.

Just as on most days, I gathered with friends in the cafeteria for lunch. While we were eating, and in between conversations, I overhead a nearby table of fellow students talking about Friday night's accident.

"It sounds creepy to me," one kid said. "Somebody said that they heard that Gwen just touched the woman, and she died."

"What? Really?" asked one of the girl's at the table.

"Wouldn't surprise me," he said. "You remember what they said about her and her brother? Supposedly, she wouldn't let go of her hold on his body when they tried to pull her out of the wreck."

"Shh!" A girl at the table harshly whispered. "Scott's sitting at the table behind you."

Ben stared at me from across the table as my jaw tightened.

"Let it go, man," he warned. "You can't stop people from talkin'."

I slowly turned around and stared at the back of the kid's head who'd been talking about Gwen.

"Sorry, Scott," said the girl at the table. "No offense or anything."

I think that her name was Becky or something. She looked fairly apologetic, and I noticed that the mouthy kid with his back turned to me fell silent.

"Yeah, whatever," I gruffly replied.

Before I turned back around, my eyes met Crissy's, one of our cheerleaders who was sitting at a table next to the one I was focused on. By the look on her face, I think that she'd heard the conversation, as well.

She gave me a sympathetic look and cast a reproving frown at the kid sitting behind me.

Honestly, everyone's hushed whispers and rumors about Gwen really pissed me off. In fact, I wanted to punch the guy at the table behind us. If he only knew what I knew about both of the accidents, maybe he wouldn't be so mouthy about Gwen.

But those were secrets that I promised Dr. Webber not to reveal.

Suddenly, the burden of my secrecy started to weigh upon me in a small way, and I wondered how frequently similar events might occur in the future.

"Blackstone, ya' better shovel that pizza down and chew later," Ben razzed. "We gotta' head to class in ten minutes or so."

In the hallway, Crissy caught up to me as I proceeded to my next class.

"I heard what they were saying in the cafeteria," she said. "I tried to tell you that day at Rushmore Burgers, remember? People talk about Gwen. There's not a lot to talk about around here, so it's like a town pastime or something."

"Well, I don't like it," I said. "It makes me angry."

She placed a supportive hand on my back.

"I'm sure it does," she said. "Don't let it get to you. Try to ignore them. You're a really great guy and I'd hate to see it eat you up inside."

"What's your take on Gwen?" I asked.

She shrugged. "I don't know. She's always seemed a little strange, but maybe that was just because of what everyone else said about her. But then, I guess she can't be all that bad if you're dating her. You have a pretty good reputation around here, I'd say. At least, people respect you."

"Thanks," I said, glancing over to see the look of sincerity on her face.

"Crissy! Hurry up or we're going to be late for fifth hour!" called one of the other cheerleaders from the opposite end of the hallway.

Crissy grinned at me and hurried after her friend. I

picked up my pace a little bit, too. It seemed like I was always in a hurry to get somewhere or to get something else done.

* * *

The remainder of the week passed quickly, though part of that was because of all of the homework assignments, including an American History essay on the Five Civilized Tribes. Then, of course, football practice really kicked my butt because Coach Lambert wanted us in good shape for Friday's home game against the Douglas Patriots, another major rival.

One thing about practice, it helped me work off a lot of nervous energy.

I texted back and forth with Gwen, but didn't have the opportunity to see her, though we did chat on the phone later in the evening. I wanted to spend time with her again, and I hoped that we'd have most of Saturday together.

She said that she had a surprise for me but wouldn't tell me anything about it. To say that I was curious was an understatement.

However, I decided that I would have a surprise for her, too. I just hoped she would like it.

By Friday, it was time for our game against Douglas and I was more than amped up and ready.

As one might expect from a team called the Patriots, their colors were red, white, and blue. Between their team colors and their color-waving fans that had showed up in town to support their team, it felt like we were playing against the United States, given our own purple and gold.

As we took the field, I glanced up to the stands to see Gwen, her mother, and my parents sitting together, which bolstered my confidence. I was struck by how much it meant to me that Gwen attended my games.

"Quit making eyes at your girl, Blackstone," Ben teased.

"Hey, yours is in the stands, too," I said.

"Yeah, but business first, man," he said. "Business first."

He had a point.

The Patriots appeared to be as pumped up about the game as we were. We were supposed to get the ball first on kickoff, but they forced a turnover after our receiver caught it and fumbled it around our eighteen-yard line. That put us defensive players in a bad situation right at the start.

We held them to three downs, but they still managed to get a field goal on us. On the succeeding return, our receiver held onto the ball and our offense worked their way down the field to trade off with our own field goal.

The remainder of the first quarter was a back-and-forth between offenses with neither team managing to keep the upper hand for more than a series or two. But the Patriots had scored two touchdowns and a field goal against our touchdown and field goal by half-time. We were all feeling pretty winded by the time we hit the locker rooms to hear our coach's half-time adjustments. Still, being down by only seven made us feel like we were still in the game.

During the second half, we were able to have better luck on defense by doing a better job shutting down the Patriots' running game. That made them fairly one-dimensional as they had to resort to a throwing game.

Fortunately, between Ben, our cornerbacks, and me, the Patriots' throwing game didn't result in many first downs and only one touchdown, and a nearly mid-field field goal by the fourth quarter. Meanwhile, our offense claimed two touchdowns and two short-range field goals, giving us an overall three point lead in the game.

The fourth quarter was an adrenaline-laced shootout between quarterbacks as each side tried to match up with their receivers. Our offense was on the field and trying for a first down with only a yard to go on fourth down.

Coach Lambert was showing some gutsy confidence in our running back, Sturm.

From the sideline, I looked up into the stands to see Gwen staring back at me with a big smile on her face. She waved and blew me a quick kiss, which made me grin from ear-to-ear.

Then I heard a collective groan from our side of the field.

"Blackstone, get in there!" I heard someone yell.

Our fourth down and a yard run attempt had failed.

I rushed out onto the field and looked up at the game clock. There were only three minutes left and the Patriots were taking over on downs from their own thirty-five yard line. All that they needed was to work their way down the field for a field goal to tie things up, or worse, a touchdown to pull ahead.

Our defense held the Patriots offense to short yardage plays on their drive, but they still managed to work their way progressively down the field to our twenty-eight yard line.

Even though they lined up in their run formation, I still remained focused on the receiver who ran in my direction. I looked over my shoulder just in time to see the football sailing toward the receiver and me.

In a vain attempt, I stretched out my hands and felt the ball impact my fingertips. Somehow, I managed to haul it in as the receiver simultaneously batted at my arms.

I was able to plant my right foot and break away from the receiver, and then I got turned downfield and barreled forward. Immediately, my fellow players began blocking for me. The crowd went wild as I dodged a Patriot tight end and offensive tackle.

As I ran further downfield, I headed down the length of the sideline, fully concentrating on the end zone ahead of me. I felt a hand grasp for my right shoulder pad but it fell away before getting a good grip. Somehow, I kept my balance and didn't step out of bounds as I continued my run.

A player sailed at my feet, nearly knocking me down, but I managed to fall across the goal line and into the end zone. Fortunately, I also maintained control of the football.

Touchdown!

Ben whooped and yelled as he ran past me, slapping me on the back as he passed by. Two other teammates grabbed me by the shoulder pads and half-hauled me to our sidelines as the kicking team sprinted out onto the field.

"Way to go, Scott!" Gwen screamed from the stands.

Turning to look up at her with a grin, she screamed down at me while clapping. My parents were shouting at me from beside her.

It was an amazing and uplifting feeling that surged through me. I felt like I could do no wrong at that moment.

The coach made his way in my direction and shouted, "That's how to get it done, Blackstone!"

We held onto the lead through the remainder of the game, adding yet another win to our record. Better yet, it was a win against a big school rival.

I was on an emotional high for the remainder of the night.

My parents, Gwen, her mother and I all went out to eat after the game, and a number of people stopped to congratulate me on my key interception.

My life felt nothing short of phenomenal!

* * *

I awoke Saturday morning feeling incredibly sore, and yet, still stoked from my touchdown and my team's victory over Douglas. My weekend was homework-free for the most part, which always felt good. Better yet, I had almost a full day set aside to spend time with Gwen.

After a quick workout to loosen up my sore muscles, I changed into jeans and a sweatshirt and then located a small gift box that was located in our attic with the wrapping paper and other accessories. I neatly arranged Gwen's gift in the box, texted her, and headed over to her house by noon.

When I pulled up in Gwen's driveway, I noticed that Dr. Webber was carrying two small plant pots, one in each hand, toward the densely-populated line of trees along one side of the properly. Though I had no idea what the plants were, each appeared wilted and brown.

As I walked around the front of my Blazer, she held up one of the small pots and shook her head.

"Gwen's trying, at least," she called out.

Then I heard the front door open and I turned to see Gwen standing on the porch.

"Hey," she said with a small wave of one hand.

She looked completely adorable when she did that.

I walked over to her and she immediately threw her arms around my waist and pulled her body against mine. As I wrapped my arms around her, I inhaled, smelling the telltale scent of herbal shampoo and a flowery-smelling perfume.

It felt so good to hold her in my arms that I could have stood there all day, actually.

"Guess what?" she asked.

I had a feeling that I knew what she was going to tell me, but I decided not to spoil it for her.

"You made luggage out of Chewie?" I asked.

She pulled away from me with a shocked expression on her face.

"No way!" she admonished and reached up under my sweatshirt to pinch at my stomach.

"Hey!" I laughed, deftly gripping her wrists in my hands.

She playfully struggled until I wrapped one arm around her waist and flung her, head down, over my right shoulder.

"No fair!" she yelped while wildly kicking her legs in the air.

I jumped up and down a couple of times with her over my shoulder and spun her around twice.

"Stop or I'll hurl all over you!" she half-shouted, half-giggled.

"She will, too," Dr. Webber quipped as she walked back with the two empty ceramic plant pots.

"Better not," I warned, quickly setting her down.

She grabbed onto my arm with both hands as she staggered slightly.

"Brute," she admonished, stifling a small belch.

I chuckled as her mother squeezed past us to go back

inside the house.

"Come with me. I have a surprise for you," Gwen said enthusiastically.

She took me by the hand and led me across the lawn to the side of the house.

As the back yard came into view, I saw a series of small to medium-sized circles of dead grass around the outlying edge of the yard where the grass met wild growth. It looked like someone had erratically sprayed weed killer in spots.

"I've been practicing," she said with a grand sweep of her arm before her.

While impressed that she had kept to her word about practicing, I felt dubious given the numerous dead patches of grass and weeds.

"Great," I supportively congratulated her.

"Um, they're really more like a lot of little failures," she conceded. "But, Mom's been very patient with me and I've managed keep the damage minimal. I practiced on a couple of small house plants just before you arrived today, in fact."

"Uh-huh," I said with a nod, recalling the two plants that her mom had been carrying.

Well, it's a start, right?

Frankly, Gwen seemed very upbeat for the most part, which surprised me.

"I'm very proud of her," Gwen's mother said as she exited the back door of the house to step outside. "She's been practicing more heavily today, so please pardon her; the euphoria hasn't worn off yet."

"Euphoria?" I asked.

"After frequently channeling our abilities, whether by giving or taking, it generates a feeling of euphoria for a short time afterward. It will last longer for Gwen because she's been at it for the past couple of hours. Still, she's making tremendous progress with the basic exercises," Dr. Webber said.

"I'm trying," Gwen offered as she reached out to hold my hand in hers.

I supportively squeezed her hand.

"I'm proud of you," I offered.

Then I remembered something.

"Are you in the mood to open something?" I asked.

"Like a gift, maybe? For me?" she asked.

I led her back to the front yard to the Blazer, fully appreciating the curious expression on her face.

"Close your eyes and hold out your hands," I said.

She closed her eyes with a smirk and expectantly held her palms up before her.

"If it's something gross, like a lizard or something, I'm going to throw it at you," she warned.

"This from the girl who has a pet *alligator*?" I countered.

"Shut up," she teased. "Now, gimme, gimme."

I placed the blue foil-wrapped box in her hands.

She opened her eyes to stare at the gift in her hands and then she glanced up at me with a curious expression.

"I hope you like it," I said with a wink.

I followed her over to her front porch where she sat on the top step and unwrapped the gift in a flurry of movements.

When she opened the lid to reveal the contents, I heard her inhale sharply.

She stood as she unfolded the purple and gold jersey and held it before her as if it were some sort of royal mantle. In reality, it looked more like a small tent against her shorter body frame.

"This is one of yours?"

"Yep," I replied with a grin and a shrug. "I know that it's kinda' big and everything."

She spun toward me and wrapped her arms around me in a tight hug.

"I *love* it, Scott," she said. "It means the world to me."

My arms encircled her body as she turned her face up toward mine and puckered her lips.

When our lips met, it was nearly electric. Her soft lips pressed against mine as I briefly drew in her sweet breath. I lingered a moment longer before pulling away. I quickly imparted an additional kiss to her.

She was an awesome kisser.

As she smiled up at me, it felt as is something very important had just been quietly solidified.

"Glad that you liked it," I said.

"Yes to both," she whispered, and unwound her arms from around me so that she could unfold the jersey before her.

"Though I'll probably end up looking like a kite or wind sail once it's on me," she added.

"I'll be sure to tie twine around your ankle on windy days," I quipped.

She playfully punched my arm.

Inside the house, she made lunch for us. We ate while perched atop her favorite pond-side spot, the partially buried boulder, as Neko Case's "I'm An Animal" played on the portable speakers next to us.

It felt great just to bask in the sun in silence while sitting next to Gwen; just being near her made me feel happy.

I glanced sidelong at her as I finished my sandwich, and she appeared to have a sullen expression on her face.

"Gwen, is everything okay? What's the matter?" I asked.

"You've been so wonderful to me, and things are going so well between us," she said. "But I think that I should be honest with you about something...about the person that I really am. I'm not a good person, Scott."

Her ominous tone concerned me.

"That's not true," I said. "Your mom explained everything to me already."

"Did she tell you that when I was a little girl, I killed my little brother right after our accident?" she quietly asked. "I only know how to kill people, Scott. Just like that woman from the accident."

I stared into her eyes and saw the pain reflected in them.

"That's not true, Gwen," I firmly stated as I held her hands in mine. "As for your brother, your mother told me that you were unable to control something inside of you that you barely even understood. She said that you tried to help your little brother, but you didn't have any training. It was an accident, Gwen, and you don't have any right to hate yourself over that."

She inhaled a deep breath and looked away.

I reached up to gently grasp her chin in my hand and I rotated her head until she looked at me again.

"And as for that lady, Sally, what you did was the only humane thing that you could do under the circumstances. She was in horrible pain and there was nothing that anyone else could have done for her."

Tears formed in the corners of her eyes, and I pulled her against me in a firm embrace.

"You are not a bad person, Gwen," I said. "You're a wonderful person, and I adore everything about you."

"Except for Mom, nobody else has ever told me that before," she said, softly crying.

I wished that I had the power to take away her emotional pain and self-doubt. Instead, I remained silent and simply held her in my arms for a time.

Eventually, she rotated her body with her back against me and I wrapped both of my arms around her.

"The funeral for that woman from the accident is today," Gwen said out of the blue.

"Really? I hadn't heard," I said.

"It was in the Custer newsletter that was emailed out this week," she said. "I sent a flower arrangement to her funeral service. It seemed like the least that I could do."

I glanced sidelong at her.

"I know you mean well, but I just don't know if that was such a good idea, Gwen," I said.

"Why not?" she asked.

"That guy, Lester, her boyfriend, was really angry," I recalled. "It might have been better just to leave well enough alone."

"C'mon, Scott, don't be so paranoid," she chastised. "If I was a member of her family, I'd probably appreciate the gesture. A lot of people in Custer did some really kind things for my mom and I, after my dad and brother died."

Instead of pressing the issue and risking starting an argument, I let the topic drop. Soon, my thoughts drifted; wandering from the dead patches of grass I'd seen that day to memories of Gwen's abilities that'd been demonstrated on the night of the accident.

I'm dating a Reaper, I silently marveled.

CHAPTER 15

I had enjoyed a great day with Gwen. I didn't leave her house until late Saturday evening, and I didn't go to bed until sometime after midnight.

However, I didn't get to sleep for very long. I was awoken in the middle of the night by my cell phone.

It was Gwen.

She sounded a little unnerved, and told me that someone on a motorcycle had just ridden up in front of their house and burned tire tread marks onto their driveway. Then they tore up the lawn by doing donuts in their yard before speeding away.

"Just one person?" I asked. "It was probably just a prank or something."

"Mom said that same thing," Gwen agreed. "It just really bothered me. Nobody's ever done anything like that before."

"Do you want me to come over?" I asked as I glanced at my alarm clock.

It was almost three o'clock in the morning.

Gwen sighed.

"No, that's okay," she said. "Whoever it was is gone now. It kind of shook me up, so I just wanted to talk, that's all."

I stretched out in my bed, idly chatting with her on

topics ranging from movies to music to what we would do if there was a zombie apocalypse.

Oddly, it occurred to us both that her talent with taking life energy would be virtually useless against the undead.

It ended up being a really weird conversation.

Around five o'clock, we said goodbye, and I rolled over and fell soundly asleep. However, I had a bizarre dream that woke me up about zombies invading our high school. One of the zombies had been Sally, the woman who'd died in the accident. Fortunately, I was so tired, I was able to fall asleep again relatively quickly.

I slept until almost noon on Sunday. By the time I completed what felt like an endless series of homework assignments, the day was nearly over. I also helped my dad rearrange the contents of our shed so that he could make room for a used snow blower he'd bought from one of our neighbors.

"They don't get that much snow around here, Dad," I teased him, as Mom came out to see what we were up to.

"Shelby, the guy up the street who sold me the blower, just bought a new one and suggested it would be handy for me to have one just in case," Dad replied. "He said that we can get some freak snowfall around here sometimes. Apparently, there'd been some terrible snowpack up in Lead back in 2011."

I just shook my head at him as Mom rolled her eyes.

"Boys and their toys," she said.

"You'll thank me in January," he assured us.

I didn't have the heart to tell him that one of my teachers at school said that, while very cold, Custer received less than fourteen inches of snow per winter.

That night, I called Gwen, and she sounded much more upbeat. She said she'd managed not to kill some of her mother's plants that afternoon.

I loved the sense of hopefulness in her voice, and I hoped that it boded well for her over the long term. It really bothered me that she hated herself for what had happened to her brother so many years ago. I didn't think that anyone deserved that level of guilt for something that was wholly out of their control.

However, by one a.m., my cell phone rang, and the encouraging tone of hopefulness in Gwen's voice had changed once more to fear.

"That person on the motorcycle is back again," she said. "I can hear him out near the end of our driveway and I think that I see the glow from his headlight through the trees."

"Is your mom home?" I asked.

"No," she replied. "She got an emergency call to see one of her patients about two hours ago. I'm not sure when she's coming home."

"Stay where you are, and don't go outside," I said. "Call the cops if he comes near your house. I'm on my way."

There was no way that I was going to let Gwen be terrorized by some jerk.

I hastily slipped into my jeans and a T-shirt and grabbed my jacket on the way downstairs. Fortunately, my parents had already gone to bed so I didn't have to explain why I was leaving the house so late on a school night.

Frankly, I didn't think that they would appreciate or understand my need to go to Gwen's house.

On the way to the front door, I grabbed the aluminum baseball bat from inside of the coat closet. Then I quietly slipped outside, locking the front door behind me.

Minutes later, I was speeding through Custer's deserted streets, completely ignoring stop signs since there was virtually nobody else out at that late hour.

I gunned the engine on my Blazer as I exited the city limits. I wasn't certain who might be harassing Gwen, but I'll admit that the guy from the accident, Lester, came to mind. Whoever it was, I was going make sure that they stopped.

Five minutes later, I squealed my tires turning south onto the county road leading to Gwen's house. I sped down the stretch of road until I saw a single headlight in the distance.

As I drew closer, the headlight turned away from me,

and the motorcycle sped southward.

"Oh no," I growled. "It's not gonna' be that easy, pal."

I increased speed as I pursued the cyclist down the bumpy country road, but I was failing to draw closer to whoever it was.

The road was fairly straight for the most part until I came upon some abrupt curves. The Blazer handled pretty well, but I had to slow down once I came upon a somewhat sharper curve in the road. My tires squealed a little bit, but I managed to remain in control.

Unfortunately, the cyclist used that opportunity to pull further ahead of me. I sped up on the straightaway past the curve, but even getting up to ninety miles an hour failed to help me catch up to him. In fact, at times I could barely see the red hue from his tail light.

After about five more minutes of unsuccessfully trying to make up the distance between us, I decided to let him go. Maybe I had scared him enough that he wouldn't come back again.

Time would tell.

I called Gwen on what seemed like a long drive back to her house, and pulled into the driveway just short of two o'clock. I noticed that her mom's Escalade was parked in front of their garage.

Both Gwen and her mom were standing on the front porch looking at me with expectant expressions.

"I chased him south for a ways, but I couldn't catch up with him," I said as I walked up onto the porch to hug Gwen. "At least they knew that I was after them, so maybe they'll leave you alone from now on."

"Thank you," Gwen whispered as she hugged me.

I couldn't help but notice that she was wearing the football jersey that I had given her. I chuckled at how it draped from beneath her jacket and well past her knees.

"That was very kind of you, Scott," Dr. Webber said. "But you shouldn't have gone after them. You could've had an accident, or worse."

I tried not to wince from the mild admonition.

Parents.

I remained quiet and politely smiled at her from over the top of Gwen's head.

There wasn't anything that I wouldn't be willing to do for Gwen. Despite her strange abilities with life energy, or whatever it was, she still seemed to be so vulnerable. Not to mention that I had grown to care for her very deeply; much more than anyone else I'd ever dated.

* * *

Despite the lack of sleep from the early morning exploits, Monday went well for the most part. I had a great football practice session during late afternoon to prepare for Friday's final game of the regular season against the Hill City Rangers. Halfway through practice, I noticed that Gwen was sitting in the stands watching me. She gave one of her cute, half-waves to me and then returned to reading her Kindle.

"Well, whadda' ya' know," Ben teased. "There's the first and only member of the Blackstone fan club."

That led to some additional razzing from more of my teammates.

After practice, I met Gwen at the edge of the field for some very welcome kissing.

"This is the perfect way to end a practice session," I said.

She giggled.

"I just wanted to thank my knight in shining armor for coming to my rescue last night," she said with a smile. "I really appreciate it."

"My pleasure," I said.

Then her expression turned serious.

"We found a lot of broken glass from shattered beer bottles near the end of my driveway along the street," she said. "It kind of freaked me out because someone might have been sitting out in front of our house for some time."

"Don't worry," I reassured her. "If you see or hear

anything else, all that you have to do is call me and I'll be there."

"Thanks, Scott," she said. "Aside from Mom, I haven't felt like anyone else has been looking out for me in such a long time."

She followed that with another series of warm, soft kisses.

It was the perfect end to my day.

However, once I got home that evening, my perfect day quickly tanked.

Once again, life was being fickle.

Neither of my parents was very pleased with me when I got home. Mom and Dad found out about my Sunday night exploits from a passing comment that Dr. Webber had made to mom that day at the hospital. Needless to say, I could sense trouble in the air.

"Just what were you thinking trying to chase someone down in the middle of the night?" Mom demanded. "Not to mention that you snuck out of the house without telling us."

"Your mother and I are very disappointed in you, Scott," Dad chimed in.

What could I say in my defense? The fact remained that I'd wanted to help look out for Gwen. Granted, the police might have done the same thing, but it was hard to just tell your girlfriend to call someone else when you could do something yourself.

"I wasn't trying to disappoint you," I began. "But I wanted to go over to comfort Gwen, and when I saw that the person was still there, well..."

"And what, exactly, would you have done if you'd actually caught the person?" Dad asked. "What if they had been armed with a gun or something? Were you prepared for those circumstances?"

Dad made a good point. I hadn't really considered that.

"Not exactly, I guess," I replied with a shrug.

"You *guess?*" Dad asked. "From now on, try thinking with your head instead of reacting solely based upon your emotions."

"Promise us that you won't do something irresponsible like that again," Mom insisted. "When Dr. Webber mentioned what had happened, I thought that I was going to choke."

I nodded, though sometimes it seemed like my mom had a tendency to be a little melodramatic.

"I promise," I said.

What else could I say? After all, saying 'no' wasn't exactly what they wanted to hear from me.

The uncomfortable silence that followed bothered me more than their admonishment. My parents glanced at each other as if they were each silently wagering who would speak next.

"This is your only warning, Scott," Dad ominously stated. "I don't want for us to have to confront this issue again with you. You're a smart young man with a promising future. You have to think things out and not jump to actions or conclusions. A key aspect of maturing is acting responsibly, and a large part of that includes thinking logically before you act."

"I understand," I said. "It won't happen again."

Mom's slightly relieved expression spoke volumes about their concern. It must have really bothered her.

I hated to feel like I'd disappointed my parents and I hoped that I wouldn't be faced again with something like what had happened last night.

Maybe I'd made a rash decision to go after the person on the motorcycle. But how could I have done any less to help Gwen?

More to the point, what would I do next time if it *did* happen again?

* * *

Thankfully, the remainder of the week passed without further incident, and Sunday night's disruption at Gwen's house seemed more and more like an isolated event as each day passed. As such, I focused my energy on the defensive plan for Friday's away game against the Hill City Rangers.

Early Friday evening, the team loaded into the bus for the short drive to Hill City, about fourteen miles north of Custer via interstate highway. Not surprisingly, the entire town was decked out in the Rangers' colors. There were green and gold banners or pennants nearly everywhere that you looked.

Fortunately, a sizeable group of Custer's residents made the drive to Hill City with us, so it felt almost as good as a home game for us.

Though technically a regular season game, there was playoff intensity in the air because both teams wanted to finish their season with a win. For us, a win meant ending the season with only one loss going into the state playoffs, making it a must-win game.

When our team went out onto the field for pregame stretches, I happily observed that Gwen and her mother were seated in the stands next to my parents.

On our way back into the locker room for a pregame talk from Coach Lambert, I looked up at Gwen and waved to her. Then Ben grabbed me by the shoulder pads.

"Man, stop that googly-eyes business," he half-teased, half-admonished. "We got us a big game to play here, Romeo!"

After the coach's pregame pep talk riled us up even more, we finally took the field just before kick-off. I felt like I was ready to light up the first Rangers receiver that tried to get past me.

It turned out that I didn't have to wait very long.

The Rangers got the ball first and their quarterback tested both Ben and me on first and second downs with deep passes to his receivers. Fortunately, we either batted down the ball or broke up the catch, denying either receiver of the satisfaction. Our defensive line also did a great job of curtailing their running game.

By the end of the first quarter, our offense had scored a field goal and a touchdown for a lead of ten to zero. Our fans were full of energy and it juiced everyone on our team with both pride and confidence.

The second quarter passed quickly with both teams struggling to establish a running game. We held the Rangers to two field goals and our offense handily made another touchdown and field goal for a twenty to six half-time lead.

It felt as if we were unstoppable.

When the game resumed after half-time, our offense took the field, but went three and out. Our punt resulted in Rangers return for a touchdown, which took some of the emotional wind out of our sails.

But our offense responded by burning up over four minutes of the clock, capping off their efforts with a touchdown. Following the ensuing kickoff, the Rangers offense began their own drive with a fake handoff to their running back and a deep pass to an open receiver in my zone of the field.

But I had been closely watching their quarterback the entire time, and I sprang into the receiver's pattern at the last moment to cleanly intercept the football. My foot slipped, but I managed to turn downfield for a thirty yard run before being tackled from behind.

Ben ran up to me and hoisted me up from the ground as our fans went crazy!

While quickly jogging back to the sidelines as our offense ran out onto the field, I laughed when I saw Gwen screaming and wildly waving our team pennants with the rest of the crowd.

Our offense was stoked, and two plays later, our running back, Sturm, bolted through the Rangers defensive line and into the end zone for a touchdown.

The score was thirty-four to thirteen by the start of the fourth quarter, and it seemed as if victory was inevitable.

I barely registered the passing of the fourth quarter as mistake after mistake plagued the Rangers, both on offense and defense; muffed handoffs to their running back, missed tackles, and a completely demoralized defense.

By game's end, Ben and I each garnered additional interceptions during desperate, last-effort passes. The Rangers only managed a single field goal in the fourth quarter, while our offense scored another two touchdowns, ending the game with a forty-eight to sixteen victory.

It was an amazing game for us!

We ended the season with a record of five wins and one loss, which gave us a strong positing starting out in the state playoff bracket. The season ended far better than I could have imagined back in August.

Between the memorable season and my relationship with Gwen, moving to Custer had changed my life for the better in ways than I couldn't have imagined.

After the game, Coach Lambert didn't waste any time getting us loaded back onto the bus. We returned to our field house in Custer to a parking lot full of classmates and townspeople. I hit the showers and changed into jeans and a clean jersey. Happily, Gwen, her mother, and my parents were waiting in the parking lot for me.

There was a huge celebration for our victory, including grilled burgers and hot dogs, as well as trays of food that covered nearly a dozen folding tables. It was an impromptu feast, to say the least.

"You were amazing," Gwen complimented me as we sat at a table together. "I'm so proud of you."

"So, are you a dedicated football fan now?" I asked.

"Only if you're playing," she replied.

She leaned against me and I wrapped one arm around her shoulders, pulling her close to me as we ate. Despite a slight chill in the night air, everything felt absolutely perfect.

After an hour or so, people started slowly leaving the gathering as a number of the adult sponsors began breaking down tables, chairs, and the grilling area.

My parents and Gwen's mom left soon afterward, leaving Gwen and me to visit with some of my teammates and their girlfriends. Before long, some of the cheerleaders made their way over to our table.

"Hey, way to go, Scott," Crissy congratulated me. "You had a great game tonight!"

"Thanks, Crissy," I said. "With the cheer squad on overdrive, who couldn't have won?"

"Mega-goober response," Gwen muttered.

Crissy chuckled as she tentatively glanced at Gwen.

"We're planning a get-together for the team tomorrow night at Stockade Lake. We're using some of the money from our summer fundraiser to buy food and drinks, but donations of anything are welcome," she said. "Will you and Gwen be able to make it out there?"

I glanced over at Gwen and she shrugged.

"Sure," she agreed.

It was nice to see her finally emerging from her social shell a little bit more.

"We'll be there," I affirmed. "Maybe I can even get my dad to donate some groceries."

Crissy smiled. "That'd be great! It starts at five o'clock. Check your email tomorrow morning and we should have the exact location picked out."

As Crissy made her way to another tableful of players, I discreetly kissed Gwen on the cheek.

"Are you sure that you're okay with going?" I whispered.

"Why not," she said with a shrug. "I'll even try not to suck the life out of the party," she added with a mock-evil grin.

I groaned and shook my head.

CHAPTER 16

As expected, my entire body was sore when I woke up Saturday morning, so I took an hour or so to do some stretches and a brief cardio workout. Afterward, I read an email from Crissy indicating that everyone was supposed to meet at a picnic area on the south side of the lake, which then reminded me about my offer to bring additional food to the event.

Fortunately, Dad was very supportive of the idea. In exchange, I helped him with inventory and stocking at the grocery store for a few hours. Before I knew it, it was already late afternoon.

I offered to pick Gwen up, but she said that she wanted to meet me out at the lake just in case she decided to leave earlier than I did. I worried that she would chicken out and not come at all, but she assured me that she'd be there.

It was nearly half past five when I made it out to the picnic area, and it appeared that most of the football team and their dates had already arrived.

As I opened the back of the Blazer, I spotted Ben and his girlfriend, Carolyn, near a picnic table with some of my fellow defensive players.

"Hey!" I shouted. "I've got a load of food over here, and 'he that doesn't help haul shall not eat'!"

A line of players quickly formed at the back of my SUV and I handed off boxes, grocery bags, and an ice-filled cooler as fast as I could. In the end, I handed a last bag of hamburger buns to an amused-looking Crissy.

"Now that's what I call killer leadership skills," she complimented me with a grin.

I shrugged.

"Food's a great motivator for football players," I said.

"I noticed," she said. "Thanks for bringing so much. We'll have way more than enough now."

"My dad's amazing," I said.

"Well, please tell your dad that we sincerely appreciate it."

"No problem," I said. "And, hey, thanks for including Gwen in this. I think it really helps for her to socialize more."

"I understand. But just between you and me, a couple of the girls weren't real happy with me over inviting Gwen. Don't worry; I warned the girls to be 'friendly and welcoming' so nobody will cause any problems," she said. "You know, I can see how good you two are together, and I'm very happy for you. Both of you."

"Thanks, Crissy," I said. "That means a lot to me."

Crissy frowned. "Speaking of which, where is Gwen? I thought that you might be bringing her."

"She said that she'd meet me here," I replied as I scanned the parking lot.

More vehicles were pulling up, but not Gwen's SUV. I texted her twice, and then wandered through the crowd chatting with people, but kept glancing at my watch and the parking lot.

Nearly half an hour later, I spotted Gwen's SUV pulling into the parking lot. Her vehicle had barely come to a stop not far from my Blazer when I received a text message.

Motorcycle following me.

I heard the sound of a motorcycle idling in the distance as I purposefully walked across the picnic area toward the parking lot.

"Hey, Scott, everything okay?" Ben asked with concern.

"Somebody on a cycle is stalking Gwen," I growled.

Ben turned to some of the players standing nearby.

"Wildcats! Somebody's bothering one of our own," he announced.

I glanced over my shoulder to see that Ben and about ten other players were following me to the parking lot.

Gwen appeared from between two vehicles and ran into my arms.

"It's okay now," I soothed. "What happened?"

I could still hear the sound of a motorcycle engine not far away, just beyond the tree line where the parking lot entrance was.

"I didn't think much of it on my way through town, but then this black motorcycle kept following right behind me all the way to the lake," she said. "He kept revving his engine and tailgating me, but then he would fall back behind me again. I was really scared."

"Stay here," I said.

I started walking across the parking lot toward the entrance area where I heard the motorcycle.

"Be careful!" Gwen called.

Ben and the other players fanned out beside me as we picked up our pace. The cycle's engine revved and it sounded much closer. I saw the glow from a headlight peek just beyond the tree line and caught a glimpse of a rider wearing a black helmet and black leather riding gear.

"I see him!" I yelled, and took off at a dead run.

I heard my teammates following at my heels.

We were less than fifty feet away when the rider revved the cycle's engine and burned tire rubber doing a half-donut on the pavement before speeding down the road.

"Damn, we almost had him," Sutton groaned.

Ben cast a dark look at him and demanded, "Man, just how many damned motorcycles have you chased down recently?"

"Aww, shut up, Collins," he said.

A couple of the players chuckled, but I kept staring into the distance, wondering who the hell was bothering Gwen. Once again, my first thought was of the guy from the accident.

Lester-something.

To say that I was angry was an understatement.

"Does anyone know who that guy was?" VanHorn asked.

I deliberately tried to think with my head instead of reacting to my emotions, just like dad had challenged me to do, but I kept focusing on the fellow from the accident.

"Not yet," I said. "But I intend to find out."

By the time we returned to the picnic area, a lot of people were standing around waiting to find out what had happened. Gwen was surrounded by a number of girls, including Crissy and Carolyn.

Gwen looked up at me expectantly as I wrapped my arms around her.

"He took off," I said.

"Sorry to make such a scene," Gwen whispered.

"It's okay," I said, hugging her to me.

"Girlfriend, you've got nothing to apologize for," Carolyn declared. "A guy that I dated once from Hill City started stalking me last year and Ben tracked that boy down and threatened him within an inch of his life. That weirdo hasn't been seen since."

"Hey, I didn't kill anybody, either," Ben piped up.

A number of people chuckled and some wandered back toward the picnic tables.

Crissy patted Gwen on the back supportively, and said, "Come on, let's get you something to drink. Maybe you can help us with setting up the food table."

"Sure," Gwen said. "Thanks."

I smiled, relieved that despite the distraction, Gwen was still being invited into the group. I glanced back toward the entrance to the parking lot, determined to find out who the rider was.

Whoever was harassing Gwen wasn't going to get away with it for long, if I had anything to say about it.

Fortunately, the remainder of the evening went really well. Gwen seemed to have a good time, and a number of the girls socialized with her, which she appeared to enjoy. It was nearly ten o'clock when a park ranger drove by in his SUV and politely told us that we needed to break up the party.

As Gwen and I helped the group to clean up the area, I kept glancing toward the parking lot, but the mysterious cyclist didn't return. Still, I followed Gwen all the way home just to make sure she arrived safely.

* * *

It had been close to midnight when I came home from Gwen's house Saturday night, so I waited until Sunday morning to mention the motorcycle incident to my parents. They intently listened to what I told them, each casting glances at the other as I spoke.

Once I'd finished, my dad offered, "That's pretty disturbing, particularly considering what happened at Gwen's house in recent days."

"Did you call the police?" Mom asked.

"No," I replied. "But what would I have told them; that a strange motorcyclist showed up at a public park? It wasn't like anything actually happened," I insisted.

"Good point," Dad said.

"Well, he was harassing Gwen on the highway on the way to the park, right?" Mom insisted.

I shrugged. "People drive like maniacs a lot of the time. Road rage is practically a sport nowadays."

Dad frowned at me, clearly not amused by my analogy.

"Well, I don't like it," Mom said as she returned to preparing pancakes.

"I don't either," Dad chimed in.

"So, then, what should I do?" I asked.

At least they couldn't say that I didn't seek their advice on the

159

matter.

"Keep a watchful eye, and call the police if he harasses you or Gwen," Dad said. "You could at least report him for stalking."

Mom glared at him from her place at the stove, clearly unhappy.

"What?" Dad innocently asked. "What else can anyone do right now?"

Mom sighed.

"I suppose it's the best that we can suggest, under the circumstances," she said.

I had to admit that it was sensible advice. However, I would've preferred something more direct, like chase the guy down the next time I spotted him.

Okay, clearly that would only get me in trouble. But it would feel very satisfying.

While eating, I texted Gwen and we made plans to get together at her house after breakfast. Granted, I still had an essay due on Thursday, but at least I was caught up on my homework for Monday and Tuesday.

Have to get ready. Give me until noon.

I stifled a groan.

Nothing fancy. Just jeans n T, I replied.

Noon, she texted.

Ok, I replied.

It never ceased to amaze me how long it took a girl to get ready for even the most ordinary plans.

By noon, I once again sat with Gwen atop the boulder down near her pond. She leaned against me with her eyes closed beneath a sunny sky. There was a slight chill in the air, but in my varsity jacket and with the sun beating down, it felt tolerable.

Gwen, on the other hand, was nestled inside of a thicker winter coat, which made me chuckle.

"You're fairly thin-blooded," I observed.

"I would rather live in Florida," she said. "Or some other similarly hot place. South Dakota doesn't stay warm long enough for my taste."

"I can keep you warm," I said with a smirk.

She opened her eyes briefly and smiled. "I'm okay with that," she said.

I bent over her to press my lips against hers. Her lips were soft and sweet, and I made my kisses deliberately tender. She stroked her soft fingertips against the skin of my cheeks, pulling me to her lips more forcefully.

A dog's abrupt barking and the uneven rumble from a motorcycle's engine somewhere close to the house startled us both.

"That sounds like Dundee's bark," Gwen said, sitting up.

I glanced up to the house as the barking continued.

Gwen and I both jolted from the booming percussion of a gunshot followed by an animal's high-pitched squeal.

"Dundee!" Gwen screamed as she jumped from the boulder.

I sprang to the ground, running up the small incline toward the house as a loud, rumbling motorcycle's engine revved up. I ran like a spirit possessed, far faster than I thought I had during any of my football games.

The engine noise grew more distant as I bounded to the side of the house and carefully peered around the corner into the front yard.

I didn't see anyone and quickly ran into the front yard just as Gwen's mother bolted out onto the front porch with a wide-eyed expression.

"Was that a gunshot?" she demanded.

Gwen rounded the corner of the house, yelling, "Where's Dundee!"

A faint whimper came from the end of the driveway and I saw the prone form of Gwen's dog lying on the gravel close to the street. I immediately ran over to where the helpless bulldog lay. Blood covered the area around him, and his breathing was shallow.

"Oh, God! Oh, God!" Gwen cried as she approached Dundee.

"Gwen, no!" commanded her mother.

She rushed past Gwen to squat next to the poor animal.

Dundee shallowly whimpered as Dr. Webber's hand softly touched his stomach.

"He's fading," Dr. Webber muttered. "Get back. Far back."

I took Gwen in my arms and guided her away from her dog.

"Okay, okay," Gwen muttered, suddenly pushing against my chest with her small hands.

"What?" I asked.

"Further back," she mumbled. "Keep going."

I let Gwen lead me more than twenty feet away from her mother and dog, and then noticed that Dr. Webber appeared to be in some kind of trance.

The only sound was the rustling of the remaining leaves and tree limbs in the fall breeze.

Dundee whined slightly and then fell silent. Gwen inhaled sharply and pulled me by the arm to lead me further away from the scene before us.

"What's happening?" I asked.

"Shh," she urged. "Just watch."

That's when I noticed that the green grass around Gwen's mother and Dundee slowly grew darker and appeared to turn brown before my eyes. Some nearby small bushes also transitioned to brown and their leaves immediately fell to the ground. Two large trees some ten or more feet from Dr. Webber creaked and then their limbs seemed to droop down from their former positions. The colorful tree leaves slowly changed from their red and gold colors to brown or black and a number of them simply fell to the ground.

"That's unbelievable," I mumbled.

Dundee emitted a sudden spasm of coughing and moaned pitifully.

"We need to get him to the vet now," Dr. Webber said as she gently scooped him into her arms.

"Got it," I said, pulling the Blazer's keys from my

pocket.

I almost dropped my keys as I noticed that Dr. Webber's normally hazel eyes had turned a bright shade of blue.

"Gwen, get my purse and lock the house," Dr. Webber said as I opened the passenger side door for her.

Minutes later, we were speeding into town to the local veterinarian's office while Gwen called their office's emergency help line from the back seat.

Within the hour, Dundee was in surgery, and Gwen, her mother, and I sat in the waiting room watching two of the office's resident mascot cats chase each other around the waiting room.

I called my parents to tell them what had happened and Dr. Webber called the police to report the incident. Gwen looked almost shell-shocked as she sat silently watching the two playful cats.

Two hours later, the veterinarian, Shelly Morrison, briefed us on Dundee's condition. Fortunately, she was able to successfully remove the small-caliber bullet from his body.

"The bullet was lodged very close to Dundee's heart. I wouldn't usually expect a dog his size with that kind of injury to survive the surgery," she said. "It's definitely a miracle."

"He'll have to stay with us for a few days for observation, but I'm hopeful that he's going to be okay," Morrison said.

"Thank you, Shelly," Dr. Webber offered. "We can't thank you enough."

"Thank goodness," Gwen mumbled.

I hugged Gwen close to me and kissed her on top of her head to help comfort her.

By the time that we returned to Gwen's house, a county deputy sheriff's car was already parked in the driveway near the street.

The deputy waved at me and pointed to Gwen's concrete driveway pad, so I parked there.

"Dr. Webber, I just got a call from Sheriff Gossett," the deputy said in a slightly confused tone. "I'm not exactly sure why he was so insistent on meeting with you in person, but he should be here very soon. In the meantime, maybe you could tell me what happened."

Gwen and I recounted what we had heard and seen and then Dr. Webber gave her account; save, of course, any ˙ mention of using her abilities to stabilize Dundee's condition.

The sheriff's car pulled into Gwen's driveway less than ten minutes later. The man who got out was an older, heavyset man with a partial squint in one eye that made him appear somewhat intimidating.

"Afternoon, Olivia," he greeted Gwen's mother with a respectful nod.

"Afternoon, Boyd," she replied with a pleasant expression.

"What do we have here, Wilkins?" he asked.

As the deputy recounted what we had told him, the sheriff nodded his head occasionally and studied the immediate area where Dundee had lain.

I looked at Dr. Webber with a curious expression and she bent over to whisper into my ear.

"The sheriff was a good friend of Gwen's father, and he's sort of looked in on us from time to time over the years."

I nodded.

"Looks like you've had some sort of strange poisoning or blight affecting your growth over here, Olivia," the sheriff observed. "Been like this for very long?"

"Kind of strange, isn't it?" Dr. Webber replied. "Perhaps some chemical change in the soil?"

"You might send a sample to the Ag boys up at the university," he suggested.

"I'll do that," she replied. "Thanks, Boyd."

"Any idea who might have wanted to do something like this?" asked the sheriff as he stared down at the spot of dried blood coating the gravel.

"I'm not certain, but I think that it might have something to do with the guy from the accident that happened over a week ago," I said.

The sheriff glanced at Dr. Webber and then regarded me at length before asking, "You mean, Lester Newcomb, don't you? The fellow who lost his girlfriend?"

I shrugged. "I recall hearing that his first name was Lester," I confirmed. "But yeah, it seems logical."

"You have any evidence of that?" he asked with a cocked brow.

"No, we don't," Dr. Webber said before I could answer.

I remained quiet as the sheriff looked at Dr. Webber and nodded.

"I see," he said.

While it was true that we didn't have any actual evidence, it seemed odd that everything was happening not long after Gwen sent the flowers to the woman's funeral. And despite his drunken state, Lester had been visibly enraged at Gwen on the night of the accident.

"All that I heard was a loud motorcycle engine and then Dundee barking," Gwen explained. "Then a gunshot."

"You sure that the motor sound was from a motorcycle?" asked the deputy.

Gwen nodded.

"I'm pretty sure that it's the same one that's been following and harassing Gwen," I said.

The sheriff and the deputy exchanged glances, and then the sheriff focused his attention on Gwen.

"What kind of following and harassing?"

Gwen recounted the nights that the cycle had been around her house and the evening that she was tailgated and intimidated on the drive out to the lake.

"Newcomb drives a Ford pickup, as I recall," said the deputy. "I don't remember him owning a motorcycle but I can check the DMV database."

"We'll interview Newcomb, just the same," offered the sheriff as he hitched his thumbs on the inside of his gun belt.

"Should we be concerned?" Dr. Webber asked.

"Not necessarily, Olivia," Sheriff Gossett replied.

"Newcomb's had a previous a history with us, that's all."

"I hope that you won't mind me asking what kind of history, Boyd," Dr. Webber insisted.

"He finished serving time at the state penitentiary for armed robbery more than ten years ago," explained the sheriff. "After he got out, there was only an occasional minor offense for public intoxication. However, Sally really helped to clean Lester up over the past couple of years. He got a decent job with a body shop down south in Pringle and he's been off of our radar for some time now."

"That's got to be pretty traumatic, losing Sally in such a horrible manner," Dr. Webber suggested.

The deputy nodded and silently stared at the sheriff.

"Well, that may be true," conceded the sheriff. "But let's run this by the numbers and just say that we'd like to have a chat with him for now."

"We'll keep you updated," assured the deputy, to which the sheriff grunted and nodded his assent.

"Call us if anything else happens," said the sheriff. "And I do mean *anything*. Okay?"

Dr. Webber and Gwen both nodded.

Sheriff Gossett and Deputy Wilkins returned to their vehicles, and we stood in the driveway watching them pull out onto the road.

"Well, that's all we can do for now," Dr. Webber said with a sigh.

"But what if he comes back?" Gwen quietly asked.

I looked at Dr. Webber, who merely shrugged and said, "Don't worry; people usually reap what they sow."

CHAPTER 17

As I half-expected on Monday morning, a number of people at school were talking about both the exploits at the lake Saturday night and the reports of the attack on Gwen's dog. Not even our big Friday night win against Hill City stemmed the enthusiasm over topics related to Gwen, which irritated me to no end.

I was a little surprised that so many people had already heard about what had happened.

Word sure does spread fast in small towns.

My sense of concern was heightened by all the talk around school, and I texted Gwen throughout the day to check on her. Granted, students weren't supposed to use their cell phones during school, but I nevertheless powered mine on between classes to contact Gwen while standing at my locker.

"Sorry to hear about Gwen's dog," Amy Fields offered as she stopped by my locker before third period. "I'd be crushed if something happened to one of my puppies."

I found her dark, Goth-like outfit and makeup to be in sharp contrast to her appreciation for animal welfare, which seemed both amusing, and yet, sincere.

"Thanks," I replied. "I'd really like to get my hands on who did it."

"Yeah, well, if you catch who did it, give them an extra smash in the face for me, too," she said. "And give my best to Gwen when you see her again. Tell her I said to call me sometime, if she wants."

"Will do," I said. "On both counts."

She gave me a half-smile and made her way back into the throng of students heading to class.

Gwen promptly responded each time I texted her that afternoon. I called to chat with her just before football practice, too.

At practice, the talk was entirely football-related. All of the players were stoked about our winning season, and we were all looking forward to the first round of games in the South Dakota Boys State Playoff brackets. Earlier that afternoon, the schedule had already been set, and we were billed to play the Bennett County Warriors on Saturday afternoon.

Coach Lambert gave us a great pep talk and then we discussed the preliminary game plan. Apparently, Bennett County was no stranger to Custer. According to Ben, the Wildcats and the Warriors had exchanged wins back and forth in recent years.

We had a great practice session, including a heavy dose of drills and some time working out in the weight room.

After practice, I checked my cell phone, only to see a disturbing text message from Gwen that she had sent less than fifteen minutes prior.

Windows broken. Called the police.

I called her cell phone but didn't get an answer, so I ran out to my Blazer and practically raced over to her house.

When I pulled into her driveway, she was standing outside with her mother talking to Sheriff Gossett as two other deputies searched around her house. It appeared that two of the smaller windows on the front of the house, including the one to Gwen's bedroom, had been broken.

As I approached Gwen, the sheriff nodded at me and asked, "Scott, where are you coming from just now?"

I frowned. "Me? I hurried over here from football practice at the school," I said. "We're getting ready for Bennett County this weekend."

"Mm-hm," he grunted. "Better practice really hard from what I heard."

I seemed to have passed his initial inspection because he shifted his gaze to Gwen.

"And where were you when this happened?"

She took a deep breath and reached out to grasp my hand.

"I was in the kitchen," she began. "I heard what sounded like one of the front windows breaking so I went to check it out. Then I heard another window breaking and I got scared and called 911 while hiding in the kitchen pantry. Then I texted Scott and called my mom."

A deputy walked out of the house holding a rough-looking piece of cement in one of his latex glove-covered hands.

"This is the culprit from Gwen's bedroom room," said the deputy. "There's another one that looks a lot like it lying on the floor in the spare bedroom."

Each of us stared at the chunk of cement in silence.

"How much would you say that weighed, Walker?" asked the sheriff.

The deputy shrugged and replied, "Quite a few pounds. Darned sure enough to break a pane glass window, if thrown hard enough. I'd say the same of the other one."

"Going to be next to impossible to get a print off of that," Sheriff Gossett mused. "Gwen, did you hear anything else? Maybe someone's voice or an engine of some sort?"

"Did you hear that motorcycle again?" Dr. Webber added.

Gwen shook her heard negatively. "I heard an engine, but it wasn't nearby or anything," she replied. "I don't think it was a motorcycle, but I can't say for certain. I was just scared that people were breaking into the house or something."

She squeezed my hand tightly as she said that, and I felt

helpless just standing there holding her hand. It made me furious that I hadn't been there to protect her.

Still, what was I supposed to do, quit school and camp out at her house?

Of course, at the moment, that didn't sound like such a bad idea to me. I could take up home-schooling just as Gwen had.

Then again, I didn't think that either of my parents would be in favor of that.

"Boyd, any leads yet on who may have shot Dundee?" Dr. Webber pressed.

Deputy Walker carried the offending piece of cement to his vehicle as the sheriff appeared contemplative.

"We're checking into a lead as we speak, but I don't feel comfortable saying anything else just yet," he hedged. "In the meantime, maybe Gwen shouldn't spend time alone at home until we get to the bottom of this."

Gwen harrumphed. "I'm not going to be chased from my own house just because nobody's here with me," she challenged.

I admired her defiance, but also considered the danger she might have been in had anyone actually tried forcing their way into her house.

"I'll increase our patrols near your house in the meantime, but I'd feel a lot better knowing that you had some additional protection close at hand," Sheriff Gossett said.

"Frank's hunting rifle is still in my bedroom closet," Dr. Webber said.

"That's fine, Olivia. Do you both know how to safely fire it?" he asked.

"I do," Dr. Webber confirmed. "But I'll need to show Gwen."

Frankly, that sounded like a good idea to me.

The sheriff looked Gwen squarely in the eye and asked, "You up for that, little lady?"

Gwen slowly nodded.

"Fair enough, then. Olivia, why don't you let me help

take care of that while I'm here today," he suggested. "I'll make sure that your rifle's had a good cleaning, too."

"Thanks, Boyd," Dr. Webber said with a grateful expression.

"You better get the glass company on the phone before they close," suggested the sheriff as he followed Dr. Webber into the house.

While I felt better knowing that Gwen and her mother would have a source of protection in the house, things had taken on a much more serious aura since the weekend's events, and I was feeling even less hopeful about the prospects for a satisfying resolution.

"I think that somebody needs a shower," Gwen observed with a wrinkled nose.

"Hey, I was just at practice, you know," I said, although I lingered at her house for a time before leaving for home.

* * *

There were no other incidents through Wednesday, and I maintained a regimen of texting Gwen throughout the day. My imagination ran away with me on a number of occasions, wondering what I would do if I failed to get a timely reply from Gwen.

Rush right over to her house, school or not, I decided.

What else could I do? I cared for her too deeply to do less.

Then on Thursday afternoon following lunch, I was asked to report to the main office. When I arrived, my dad was waiting at the main desk.

"What's up? Is Gwen okay?" I asked.

"Relax," Dad said. "Everybody's fine from what I know. Sheriff Gossett merely asked if we could meet him and your mother at the Custer police station. They have some new development to discuss with us. Better grab your stuff, too. I'm not sure how long this may take."

I was curious to say the least, and I gathered my

backpack from my locker before leaving. I followed Dad's SUV to the police station, and we parked next to my mom's car. I also noticed Gwen's mother's Escalade in the parking lot.

We were directed to a small conference room where Gwen, her mother, and my mom were already seated. Sheriff Gossett and Roger McDowd, the Custer police chief, were there, as well.

"Please, have a seat," the chief offered after he and Sheriff Gossett shook hands with my dad and me.

I took a seat next to Gwen, who gave me an optimistic look and reached out to hold my hand beneath the table.

"Thank you for coming down here on short notice," Sheriff Gossett said. "This is something that the Chief and I didn't want to delay further."

"The County Sheriff's Office and the Custer Police Department have been working together on the recent investigation into the harassment of Gwen and her mother," Chief McDowd began. "Based upon field interviews and evidence that we've collected, we believe that we've identified at least one of the culprits who are involved."

I looked at Gwen expectantly, but she appeared just as puzzled as I felt.

"First, I'd like for each of you to look at some photographs that we have," said the chief as he placed pictures on the table before us.

Some of the photos were a series of similar-looking black motorcycles, as well as the faces of a number of young to middle-aged looking men wearing black leather jackets.

One of the motorcycles stood out in my mind as I held the photo.

"That's it," Gwen said while pointing to the photo in my hand. "I'd swear that's the motorcycle that was following me."

"Yeah, this looks like the cycle that we saw at the lake," I said.

I saw the chief and the sheriff exchange knowing

glances.

"How about any of the people in the photos," asked the sheriff.

I pointed to the photo of the guy who'd been at the highway accident. Lester-somebody.

"That's the guy from the accident," I said.

"Agreed," Gwen said.

"And have you seen him at any other time since the accident?" asked the chief.

Gwen and I both shook our heads.

"I see," replied the chief.

"Gentleman, what exactly are we confirming here today?" asked my dad.

"The motorcycle that Gwen and Scott recognized belongs to this gentleman," replied the sheriff as he pointed to a photo of a young, but tough-looking, man. "Pete Hampton. He's the brother of Sally Hampton; the woman who died in the accident."

"But that's not Lester Newcomb," I countered. "Isn't he the guy who's behind all of this?"

Gwen squeezed my hand in a cautionary fashion.

"That's the thing about investigations, son," Chief McDowd said. "They sometimes take you in directions that you may not have expected."

"Pete Hampton's cycle, the one that you both just identified, was found to have traces of gravel dust imbedded in the cycle's tires that match the type of dust in the gravel of Gwen's driveway," Sheriff Gossett explained.

"And you think that Hampton is responsible for everything that's happened?" Dr. Webber asked.

"Well, once we confronted him with our evidence, he confessed to going to your home at night and to following Gwen to the lake, though he claimed that he didn't mean any harm. At most, we can tie him to those broken bottles of beer that you found near the road at the end of your driveway."

"What about breaking our windows and shooting Dundee?" Dr. Webber demanded.

Chief McDowd scratched his head.

"Well, that's another thing entirely, Olivia," replied the sheriff. "Pete Hampton has a criminal record, including time in the county jail for some misdemeanors and minor felonies a few years back, including a sealed juvenile record. He's been pretty clean for the past few years since his sister, Sally, helped reform him."

I couldn't help thinking about how Sally had apparently had a positive influence in a number of people's lives, which only made her death seem that much sadder.

"Pete aside, the Hamptons are fairly respected in the community," Chief McDowd said. "Sally did a lot of community volunteer work, including reform outreach to convicted felons. That's how she met Lester Newcomb. Sally's father also does outreach and is a respected Baptist pastor down in Hot Springs, in fact."

"We don't have any hard evidence to tie Pete to either the shooting or the vandalism, but he's nervous enough about the possibility of going back to jail that he wouldn't confess unless we had something harder than circumstantial against him," said the sheriff.

"However, we do recommend that a victim's protective order is filed on Gwen's behalf against him," recommended the chief.

Dr. Webber glanced at the sheriff. "Boyd?"

"It's a good idea, Olivia," confirmed the sheriff. "A VPO will give us more leverage to act against him if we need it. In fact, I'd recommend adding your name to it, as well."

Gwen nodded at her mother.

"I'm okay with that," Dr. Webber said. "Let's proceed."

"What about Lester Newcomb?" asked my mother.

"He was on our radar at first due to the fact that he had a romantic relationship with Sally, and he was naturally very upset following the accident. We thoroughly investigated him, but no evidence ties him to any of the events," replied the sheriff. "Lester doesn't even own a motorcycle. And you've identified the cycle as the one belonging to Pete Hampton."

"Newcomb could have used Pete's motorcycle," suggested my father.

"Now that's genuine investigative thinking," offered the sheriff. "However, we thought about that, as well, particularly since Lester and Pete were mutually-acquainted through Sally. Again, there's no hard evidence, and Lester has alibis for the events in question. We were also encouraged to learn that Sally's father has been providing grief counseling to Lester, as well. Pastor Hampton spoke highly of his progress, in fact."

I considered what the sheriff said, and thought back to something my dad had recently told me.

You have to think things out and not jump to actions or conclusions.

"With luck, this will be the last trouble that you'll have with Pete Hampton," Chief McDowd said, casting glances between Gwen and her mother. "The key thing is for either of you to call us if he comes near you or your property."

Gwen regarded me with a hopeful expression and squeezed my hand, so I gave her a reassuring grin.

It was definitely odd how things had a way of working themselves out.

CHAPTER 18

By Friday, I was feeling more hopeful that events would finally return to some semblance of normal. There was a teacher's conference for the day, so school was out of session, including the cancellation of formal football practice. Still, I felt confident that I'd be ready for Saturday's game against Bennett County.

All in all, life seemed pretty good once again.

I called Gwen and we made plans to spend the afternoon together, including grilling some burgers for dinner that evening.

"Naturally, I offer the benefit of my grilling services, expertly honed and perfected from the years of watching my dad," I said.

"Oh, brother," Gwen said. "I'm sure that my mom will just be happy not to have to cook for a change."

As I drove through town on the way to Gwen's house, I caught a glimpse of Pete Hampton's black motorcycle parked in front of my family's grocery store.

It probably shouldn't have bothered me, I rationalized. Still, I felt somewhat suspicious given everything that had happened, so I whipped into the parking lot and pulled into a spot two spaces down from his cycle.

Judy, one of the cashiers, greeted me as I walked into the

store.

"Your dad's in the back storage area," she said.

I nodded as I casually headed to the back of the store, though I carefully scanned each of the aisles on my way there. As I approached the swinging doors leading into the back of the store, I noticed Pete sifting through the packages of lunchmeat in one of the meat department freezer bins.

Just laying eyes on him made my blood boil. I clenched my fists, half-tempted to walk over and punch the guy in the jaw. The aggravation that he had caused Gwen was more than enough reason for me to at least give him a black eye.

Then my father's words echoed in my mind.

...a key aspect of maturing is acting responsibly, and a large part of that includes thinking logically before you act.

At that moment, Pete looked up as he placed a package of lunchmeat into his shopping cart. I could tell by his sour expression that he immediately recognized me. We stared at each other for a few seconds, sizing each other up.

Despite his steely expression, I definitely wasn't intimidated by him.

In fact, part of me wanted so much for him to approach me; not so much so that I could report him to the police, but more so that I could take out my frustrations on his face.

While a satisfying prospect, I realized that was probably a bad idea.

As if in some silent recognition of my thoughts, Pete looked away and quickly pushed his shopping cart down a side aisle leading to the front of the store.

"Everything okay, son?" Dad asked from out of nowhere.

I started, and replied, "Huh? Oh, yeah. Everything's fine, I guess."

His expression spoke volumes, as if I had just gotten caught with my hand in a cookie jar. Instead, he quickly adopted a sober look.

"You know," he began. "One thing that I learned a long time ago was that you can't always control what happens to you in life, but you always have control over how you choose to react to it."

I nodded and thought about that for a moment, all too aware of the subtle advice he'd just imparted.

"I'll try to remember that," I replied.

"Fair enough," he said.

"Well, I better head on over to Gwen's," I said. "I probably won't be home for dinner. I'm grilling for them tonight."

"Okay," he temporized. "So, you came all the way into the store to tell me that? I thought that teens only text everybody nowadays."

"Lame, Dad," I said.

I turned to walk away.

"Hey, Scott," Dad called.

I glanced back over my shoulder at him.

He tapped his forehead with one fingertip and said, "Think first. Make me proud, son."

"Got it, Dad," I said.

"And, hey, if you're eating dinner with Gwen and her mother tonight, why don't you take something from the bakery with you," he added with a wink. "Have Judy add it to our family tab."

"Thanks," I said.

I selected a chocolate cake and noticed on my way out to the Blazer that Pete's motorcycle was already gone.

Once more proceeding through town, I called Gwen's cell to let her know that I was on my way.

"I wondered what was keeping you," she said. "I was almost catching a chill sitting down here by the pond."

"You'd catch a chill in the middle of the desert," I quipped.

"Shut up," she retorted. "You *can* catch a chill in the desert at night, you know."

Yet more arcane trivia that she pulled out of her head.

"You're too smart for your own good," I said.

"Smart is the new sexy," she said.

"Smart is okay," I remarked. "But plain old sexy is always in style."

"Now you're just being difficult," she chided. "And to think that you used to be so sweet to me."

"Hey, I've got something sweet for you when I arrive," I said.

"Mm," she murmured. "Does it involve lips by any chance?"

I chuckled.

"Actually, yes," I said. "And chocolate icing."

She groaned. "Food-related. I should have known," she said.

"Hey, I'm hoping that we can arrange the other thing, too."

"That'll be much easier with Mom not around," she said.

"Oh, really?" I said. "Will she be gone long?"

"Well, probably not for more than an hour or so," Gwen replied. "She's making a few patient rounds at the hospital."

I couldn't help but smile at the prospects of spending some exclusive quality time with Gwen.

"Hey, I can hear your truck. You made it here pretty fast," she remarked.

I frowned. "What? I'm still only halfway to your house," I said.

"Well, I better see who it is then," she said.

"Expecting anyone?" I asked.

"Just you," she said.

Moments later, I heard her curse under her breath.

"What is it? What's wrong?" I demanded.

"It's that guy from the accident," she said.

Gwen gasped. "Oh, crap, he's got a gun!" she squealed.

The roar from a gunshot sounded over the phone.

"Gwen!" I yelled.

I floored the accelerator and my Blazer's engine immediately roared to life.

"Gwen!"

The sound of Gwen's labored breathing was all that I

could hear as I swerved into the oncoming lane to go around a slower car in front of me.

"Running...pond," I managed to catch from her clipped speech.

"Gwen? Gwen, hide and call 911! I'm almost there!"

Then the line went dead, and my heart thundered in my chest. I was stunned and alternated between cursing and praying as I rounded the corner onto the county road, nearly losing control of my SUV.

"Dammit!"

I managed to maintain control of the vehicle as my mind raced, wondering what I should do. I fumbled with my phone, trying to dial 911.

"Please be okay," I pleaded.

However, an even darker fear plunged my thoughts into complete chaos as I struggled to slow down my SUV in order to safely control the sharp turn into Gwen's driveway.

An older model Ford truck was parked in front of Gwen's front porch.

I barely managed to jam my SUV into park before I burst out through the driver's side door.

What to do, I thought as I made my way to the side of the house.

At least I didn't see any blood, but I smelled the scent of burnt gunpowder in the air.

Gotta' save Gwen!

"Custer County 911. What is the nature of your emergency?" came a woman's voice over the cell phone.

It startled me.

"Look, I'm at Gwen Webber's house and somebody's trying to kill her," I managed to say. "Lester Newcomb. The guy's got a gun!"

"Can you tell me the address?" asked the woman.

Surprised that I actually remembered, I absently rattled off Gwen's address as I hurried toward the back yard from the side of the house.

Thankfully, I didn't see Gwen's body.

"Police have been dispatched," said the woman. "Find a safe location and stay on the line with me, okay? Just tell me your name."

A gunshot sounded and my eyes instantly trained on the area down near the pond. I could see that Lester Newcomb stood adjacent to the pond as he actuated the slide on a shotgun.

"Evil witch!" he yelled. "You ain't gettin' away with killin' and terrorizin' people anymore!"

"Sir? Can you hear me?" inquired the woman on the phone.

My mind felt numb and sluggish as I reasoned that I couldn't wait for the police.

I have to help Gwen now!

"Sir, are you still there?"

I ignored my cell phone and ran back to the SUV, which I belatedly realized I'd left running. I jumped into the driver's seat and slammed the vehicle into drive.

The Blazer's engine roared as I gunned the SUV onto the front lawn. Within seconds, my SUV bounced wildly down the slope behind the house leading to the pond.

I floored the accelerator.

Lester's head jerked to stare in my direction as I tightly gripped the steering wheel, barreling toward him.

He raised his shotgun to fire into my windshield but I ducked down behind the dashboard at the last second.

The windshield shattered, and I heard pellets impact into the cab and seat. I bobbed my head up in time to slam down hard on the brakes. The SUV careened and skidded to a halt at the edge of the pond.

I jerked the driver side door open, catching Lester's left shoulder with a glancing blow and knocking him to the ground.

As Lester staggered to his feet, I rolled out of the cab and threw my cell phone at him as a distraction. It bounced harmlessly off of him but I followed by slamming my right fist into the side of his temple.

The butt of the shotgun jabbed into my left side, and pain shot up through my torso. I ferociously punched at him with my right fist as I grabbed at the hot barrel of his shotgun with my left hand, burning it in the process.

Gwen screamed from somewhere close by as I wrestled with Lester over control of the shotgun. He punched at me with his left fist, catching me with a glancing blow to my jaw.

Despite the pain, I held onto the shotgun with my left hand and head-butted him with my forehead, which caused his hand to slip. I jerked with all my strength and managed to gain control of the butt-end of the shotgun.

I barely had time to set my finger against the trigger before he punched me in the face.

As I staggered backward and closed my left eye for a second where he'd punched me, the shotgun discharged toward him. The sound momentarily stunned me, but I saw him scowling back at me.

He lurched forward against me and I felt a horrible stabbing pain shoot through my body's midsection. The gun slipped from my fingers as I stared down at a large knife protruding from my upper body.

"Damn you, boy!" he yelled. "See what you went and made me do!"

I had trouble drawing a breath as my hands immediately went to the hilt of the knife.

"Scott!" Gwen screamed not far from me.

I felt my legs buckle and my body began falling to the ground. Somehow, I managed to balance myself slightly as my knees impacted the moist soil.

The pain in my body was unbearable.

Gwen suddenly appeared at my side, holding onto my shoulders with a shocked expression on her face as Lester Newcomb slowly reached down to the ground to retrieve the shotgun.

I had failed Gwen.

"Oh, no, oh, no, oh, no," Gwen rambled.

"*Run,*" I urged her in a hoarse voice.

A mixture of sharp and throbbing pain coursed through my body as I gripped the hilt of the knife and pulled with all my strength.

Blinding, searing agony ripped through me, but I felt the knife slip free from my body.

I pressed my hands to the wound and my stomach grew warm and wet as the intense pain threatened to overwhelm me.

I fell backward onto the ground as a persistent ringing in my ears overtook my hearing. The blurry form of Lester hovered on the periphery of my vision as Gwen stared down at me from above.

"*Run,*" I gasped with what little remaining breath I had in my lungs.

Then I slipped onto the ground.

I stared up into the hazy blue sky, puzzling over how the formerly unbearable pain in my gut was quickly fading into the background of my waning awareness.

Small, soft hands pressed against the sides of my face, and through the persistent buzzing in my ears, a prolonged, high-pitched scream pierced the air.

The world around me abruptly went black, even as I heard somebody yelling in the background.

Everything sounded so distant.

Then silence.

I vaguely felt a coolness wash through my body as a bright orb overtook my vision, warming me again.

It felt as if I was falling through emptiness, and I merely wanted to fall asleep.

Nothing but silence and a smothering peacefulness permeated my existence.

I faced the tantalizing promise of relief as my perception of time ceased.

Then a massive shock coursed through my body, instantaneously spurring me back to a fuller sense of consciousness; the formerly warm, bright orb of light faded into darkness.

My eyes erratically blinked, finally opening to once more reveal the hazy blue sky above me. Sounds emerged, including the lapping of water and the rustling of nearby tree branches.

The scene above me became eclipsed by Gwen's relieved-looking visage hovering above me. Her long, dark hair fell around my face like a curtain, tickling the sides of my face. The edges her lips curled upward into the beginning of a satisfied smile as she thoughtfully stared down at me with teary-looking eyes.

Strangely, leaves were falling and fluttering all around us. *Black, dead leaves.*

Then something caught my attention out of the corner of my eye, and I turned my head to stare into Lester's dark-rimmed and hollowed-looking eyes.

He lay less than a few yards away; still and gaunt, like a body that I had previously seen in horror films. It was the look of death.

"Welcome back," Gwen whispered, as she perched above me.

A sudden roar emitted to our left, startling us both.

Chewie sprang from the pond under a spray of cold water to clamp his gaping jaws onto Lester's leg. In a matter of seconds, and with a feral-sounding growl, the reptile pulled the man's body back into the pond with him.

I used what little energy I could muster and pushed myself up on my elbows to gaze at the pond and make sure that the gator didn't appear to be returning. To my amazement, the formerly unbearable pain in my body had subsided to a manageable, dull ache.

"It's okay," Gwen said as she scanned the pond. "Chewie left."

My eyes shifted to glance down at my bloody shirt. That's when I realized that I was lying within a large circle comprised of brown grass and blackened and withered plants. The dormant-looking husks of nearby trees and shrubs sagged in place around us like a grim mantle.

To my disbelief, everything within nearly a thirty-foot circular area around us appeared to be dead!

"What the---" I said.

"Don't worry, Scott," she assured me. "You're going to be okay now."

"But h-how did you---" I stammered.

She delicately placed her index finger against my lips.

"You caused me to break down the barrier I had built inside me," she said. "I was able to channel life forces to help you."

I kissed her fingertip and she withdrew it from my lips.

"And, Lester?" I pressed.

Gwen merely shrugged. "Mom always said, 'People usually reap what they sow,'" she whispered.

Slowly, the dual meanings behind her words sank into my mind.

People reaped what they sow.

And Gwen, the girl who I had completely fallen for, the young Reaper, had saved us both.

Oddly enough, I was okay with that.

Then Gwen's soft lips pressed against mine in a lengthy kiss that was amazing; simultaneously charged with veritable energy and sweetness. I kissed her back, just to make sure that I hadn't been dreaming it.

The second kiss was as amazing as the first. Perhaps even more.

"I love you, Gwen," I whispered.

If it had been the last words I ever uttered to anyone, I knew that I had to say them to her.

"I love you, too, Scott," she softly replied in an oddly reassuring tone, as tears formed in the corner of her eyes and the sounds of sirens increased from the direction of her house.

* * *

Scarcely two weeks had already passed since the incident

with Lester Newcomb as Gwen and I perched atop the boulder that she'd started referring to as 'our rock.' My stab wound was healing nicely and the lingering soreness was quite bearable, though my midsection itched where the stitches had been inserted.

"Remarkably minimal damage for such a wound," said the surgeon after I had awoken from surgery.

I glanced at the huge dead patch of black and brown-colored growth that had marked the spot of horror two weeks ago.

"More blight." This was what Gwen said that her mother had told Sheriff Gossett upon further inquiry.

Not far from the 'blighted' area, the deep ruts left from my Blazer's tires were still firmly indented in the soft soil leading to the edge of the pond. From there, my eyes scanned the surface of the glasslike surface of the water. And this time, I didn't have to wonder where Chewie might be treading.

The Reptile Gardens had been called to retrieve Chewie during the recovery of Lester's floating remains.

Lester Newcomb.

...died from an apparent heart attack during his vicious assault and attempted murder of two teens just outside the small town of Custer, the news had proclaimed.

No matter their claim, just as long as Gwen's true nature remained a secret.

I pulled her body against me with one arm, and she murmured with approval, softly patting my thigh with her hand.

"Do you miss Chewie?" I asked, dismissing the dark thoughts that lingered in my mind.

"Yeah," she said. "But after seeing him launch out of the pond like he did, it made me realize that he'd be better off with his own kind."

"You mean, we'd be *safer* if he was living at the Reptile Gardens," I suggested.

"Oh, hush," she said. "Maybe a little bit," she conceded

with a sigh. "But I bet that you've missed football just as much."

It was true. Due to my injury, I'd missed being able to play in the first game of the South Dakota Boys State Playoff Bracket. Our team had played the Bennett County Warriors as scheduled. While in the hospital, Coach Lambert had called me on game day to say that the team was dedicating the game to me.

Unfortunately, though tied at the end of regular game play, our team lost twenty-four to twenty-seven during overtime.

Isn't that just how life goes sometimes?

While the team made a strong showing in the game, I couldn't help wondering if my participation might have somehow helped us to win. I had so looked forward to playing in that game.

Still, I felt fortunate that the doctors said that I'd make a full recovery, and should even be able to play football again by the start of next season. It would definitely give me incentive during my healing process.

A cool breeze played through the trees and across our faces, leaving only the sound of rustling branches and the shifting of dry, fallen leaves.

"Amy Fields called me last night," Gwen said.

I frowned. "Yeah? What did she say?"

"Nothing important," she replied. "She just wanted to chat, that's all. We talked about our pets and a bunch of other things."

"That was nice," I said.

"Yeah, it was," Gwen said with a grin. "We had a really good chat."

I was glad to hear that. Despite her dark, Goth-like persona, Amy seemed like a really nice person, as well as somebody who might genuinely appreciate what it was like to be 'different' from everyone else.

"So, what would you think about me enrolling at the high school beginning in the spring?" Gwen asked.

I smiled and looked into her eyes.

"I think that'd be great," I said. "Are you sure, though? Even more than before, I wouldn't be surprised if you and I are hot rumor mill topics nowadays."

In truth, Ben and some of my other teammates had already tipped me off to that during some recent visits. Not having been back to school since my injury, I'd probably find out just how much when I returned on Monday.

Gwen nodded. "True," she said with a sad expression. "But I've dealt with people talking about me for years, and I think that I've spent enough time being alone."

It made me so happy to hear her say that.

I closed the short distance between us and kissed her. Then, like an addict, I kissed her again, appreciating her soft lips and the slightly electric charge that raced through my body.

In mere moments, and despite my recent near death experience, my life once again felt strangely, bizarrely complete; filled with great promise. And I felt content in the satisfaction that I had found someone very dear and special to share it with.

The grin on my face was so big that I felt almost silly, and Gwen giggled at me while soothingly caressing her fingers through my hair.

I adored the sound of her giggle.

As I stared into her beautiful eyes, it occurred to me that life was indeed a spectrum of things, from pleasurable to bizarre, and even slightly twisted. Most of all, I realized that life definitely wasn't, and never would be, completely perfect.

It might, in truth, be fickle.

Yet, there was nothing either fleeting or fickle about my feelings of love for Gwen, or how strongly I relished the prospects of spending my life with her.

ABOUT THE AUTHOR

Jaz Primo: Delving into flights of fancy and realms of imagination; eagerly sharing with you.

Jaz takes great pleasure in sharing his creative visions. He's a history aficionado, "pun-master", and all-around fan of vampires. He authors paranormal romance, urban fantasy, and young adult literature, and has enjoyed a fulfilling background and career in higher education, including teaching U.S. History classes during evenings. Jaz lives in the Great American Midwest.

You can discover more about Jaz Primo online at jazprimo.com

You can find Jaz Primo online at the following locations:

Website: http://jazprimo.com

Facebook: Author Jaz Primo

Twitter: @jazprimo

Sunrise at Sunset: Revamped

Second Edition

Book One of the *Sunset Vampire Series*

by Jaz Primo

The *Sunset Vampire* series was awarded Third Place in the Reviewer's Choice Award for Best Paranormal Series of 2012 by the Paranormal Romance Guild.

With a distribution exceeding 100,000+ since its 2010 debut, the Sunset Vampire series has grown to become a favorite among vampire and paranormal romance readers. There are currently four books in the series with additional titles forthcoming.

When is a bloodthirsty predator the best protection against a psychotic killer?
When the predator is both a vampire...and the woman you love.

Caleb is bravely overcoming a dark past while having no memory of the beautiful vampire that saved him.
Despite a promise to stay away, Katrina is compelled to return to him.
However, a vengeful rival from her past has dire plans for both of them.
Can one woman's love triumph over another's thirst for revenge?

Now available in trade paperback and all major eBook formats!

Bringer of Fire

Book One of the *Logan Bringer Urban Fantasy Series*

by Jaz Primo

The twenty-first century has arrived, but the world is a darker place where international superpowers tenuously jockey for both political and economic supremacy. It's a time when the rights and interests of the individual carry little weight. But a medical breakthrough spontaneously blossoms telekinetic abilities within the body of one man, altering humanity's evolution and threatening to tip the world's balance of power. That man is Logan Bringer.

When humankind's greatest achievement leads to a race for its control, some will bring political and economic powers to bear.

Others unleash an array of assassins and weaponry.

However, when Logan's family is directly threatened, he unleashes himself.

He is...the *Bringer of Fire*.

Now available in trade paperback and all major eBook formats!

www.ingramcontent.com/pod-product-compliance
Lightning Source LLC
Chambersburg PA
CBHW070844120626
46556CB00002B/868